The Long Haul

by
N. K. Ferris

Dedication

This book is dedicated to my husband,

Rich,

who constantly encourages me to experience

new and exciting endeavors

and

to my sons, John and Kyle,

of whom I am exceedingly proud

Acknowledgment

Many people played an important role in this effort.

First, my dearest friend, Kaye, provided the story idea for this novel, helping me develop the characters and the plot. During this time, we laughed a lot and I'm grateful for her good humor and insight.

My digital professor, Josh, taught me how to use a computer and was invaluable in teaching the complexities of putting my thoughts on paper.

My favorite cousin, Mike, author of two novels, coached and prodded me to get serious.

Jan, the facilitator of a writing workshop in SaddleBrooke Ranch, along with other members of the group, who critiqued my work for two years.

Special thanks to my editor, Alexis Powers, who pushed, shoved and nagged until I believed that my work was a good read and merited publication.

Finally, thanks to Ray Hammond who pulled it all together.

An old Chinese proverb states:

"When the student is ready,
the teacher will appear."

PART I

Southern Hospitality

Chapter 1

The two flags, American and Tennessee, were snapping salutes as I bounded up the front steps of the county courthouse with my backpack. The morning sky was crystal blue on a day not to be wasted. Life was good in Turtle Creek.

Courthouses in the south are as different on the outside as the cases heard on the inside. Models of the Civil War era were built to last, but those built with surplus materials after World War II are shoddier. This courthouse, with a flat roof, thin gray stone siding and crumbling concrete steps, offered no aesthetic relief. The cheap windows, cloudy like rheumy eyes, reflected the decaying town square from all four sides. My zippity-do-dah day ended when I stepped inside the dark paneled interior.

* * *

I was cleaning my glasses in courtroom two when the wooden gavel pounded the podium with a sound like gunfire. Divorce Court was in session. Judge Royce Lester II presiding. Next case: Mills vs. Mills. With over thirty years on the bench as a Circuit Court Judge in middle Tennessee, Judge Lester commanded attention before he spoke. For three years I had witnessed many of his cases, spanning divorces to murders and everything in between. There I was again on the back row, A. C. King, an aspiring reporter for the local county newspaper checking for anything newsworthy. I trolled at the courthouse a lot, but had never seen a court hearing begin this way.

His Honor thundered for both lawyers to approach the bench. Before he flipped the switch for his beloved white noise machine, I heard him remark, "Six years?"

The two lawyers slowly rose from their seats, approaching the bench as if they were walking to the gallows, heads down, shoulders slumped and visibly intimidated. I could only imagine what the Judge was thinking from the disgruntled look on his face. My curiosity was aroused. This day was looking sunny again.

Shifting my attention to the plaintiffs, I studied them while the judge was having his come-to-Jesus meeting with the counselors. I had not seen the middle aged couple, Mack and Ginny Faye Mills, before today. She appeared composed, sitting straight with relaxed hands folded in her lap, but he displayed aggressive body language, leaning forward with his elbows on the table, fists interlocked under his chin. With his lips pulled together and his jaw set tight, he looked like a middleweight ready to throw a punch or have a stroke.

When the judge proceeded, he had my full attention. For an hour the attorneys argued over a ski boat, sports cars, a cabin on water front property, half a dozen rental properties and the alleged theft, by her, of his bulldozer, all reflecting money, money and more money.

This is one bizarre hearing. I shifted in my seat, squinting at my notes. I needed to know why this or any divorce would take six years and still be unsettled.

The lawyers for the couple were Phyllis Faulkner and Richard Pruitt. I Googled them while the hearing remained bogged down in accusations. Ms. Faulkner, Mack Mill's attorney, was a thirty-something, good looking woman; out of my league, but beautiful arm candy for someone. With her law degree from Vanderbilt, and a position at Banks and Sloane Law Office in Nashville, she did not come cheap. Why would a man choose a female lawyer to get a divorce, but hey, maybe Mr. Mills liked what he saw, too.

Richard Pruitt was representing the wife, Ginny Faye Mills. He owned his one-man law firm, conveniently located across the street from the courthouse. His overweight body was not used to walking far and his movements were stiff and slow. The bags under his eyes made him look much older than the image on his website. Pruitt had the same disgusted look on his face as Judge

Lester and I bet both of them couldn't wait to get this case settled and into the court records.

Obviously frustrated, Judge Lester announced a continuance of the divorce hearing, two weeks from today, June 15. He then brought the unresolved hearing to a close, announcing a recess for lunch before his next case on the docket. I made a note of the date and planned to ask my editor for a chance to 'poke a stick at a sleeping dog'. Maybe I was bored with all the ordinary news and needed to stretch my imagination, but I smelled a bigger story buried under the divorce case. A reporter has to trust his nose. With my laptop tucked safely in my backpack, I left the ugly courthouse via the side exit and headed to the Post Gazette.

* * *

Turtle Creek has four traffic lights within the city limits. Not one has a walk button. You take your life in your hands crossing at any point. Deep in thought when I stepped off the curb, a huge truck with a cruise ship horn blasted me back to reality. *Whew, close call.* A logical thought floated to the surface of my brain. I would ask the Chief of Police what he knew about the contentious couple, Mack and Ginny Faye Mills. The Chief and his cousin, the county Sheriff, knew most of the local population so maybe one of them would enlighten me.

After earning a BA in journalism at Tennessee Tech, I landed a job paying minimum wage with the local county newspaper. My parents agreed to my renting at home until I paid off my college loans and were happy to have me back. In my spare time, I read political thrillers and mysteries. Becoming a free-lance investigative reporter is my ultimate goal, but I keep a journal in case I write the great American novel someday.

Chapter 2

Each time I entered the Post Gazette, my nose was assailed with the sweet smell of ink. Intoxicating. The newspaper office looked like a messy storage building for past editions, with boxes of paper stacked along the walls and layout work in progress spread across the tables. I knocked on the door of my editor, Loretta, and presented my new idea for a story.

"What are you thinking, Ace? Divorces are not for public consumption on the front page." *Loretta was often open to odd-ball stories, but not this time.*

Not willing to give up, I said, "I know that, but I believe a back story is hiding behind this divorce from hell. Even though a special judge was assigned to find all the assets, they are still in discovery. Judge Lester knows that all the facts have not come out in that courtroom. Mack Mills is protecting something that he wants to stay hidden.

"I see your point. Six years does raise a red flag. It is ridiculous that a person can be convicted and executed in Texas in two years, but taking six years for a divorce in Tennessee, with no kids involved and all that expensive property. I bet somebody has a serious need to keep their business deals wrapped up tight."

"That's exactly what I was thinking. So can I look into it? I plan to talk with Chief Herring first and see if he knows anything about the Mills family."

"All right, Ace. You have two weeks to run with this. Report back to me. Do not waste my time." And with a back-handed wave I was dismissed.

Chapter 3

With the Police Station next door to the Post, I visit them every day for new reports on crime right here in Gotham City. Small towns don't require a car to get around so I stay in shape by walking the six blocks from home to the office and back. When I walked in, the dispatcher was yawning and filing her nails so I knew things were slow. I asked if the Chief was in, even though I could see him through the glass door to his office. She politely rang his extension while he waved me in.

Chief George Herring had a son, Ben, who died in Afghanistan. A framed photo of him in his dress blues hung behind the big desk. An American flag flanked the right side of the picture and the State flag stood on the left making me feel I should salute. Ben graduated high school four years ahead of me, going straight into the Marine Corps, where he became an MP and loved it. Chief Herring was proud of him.

The greeting was manly. "Hey, Ace."

"Hey, Chief," I said back.

My initials, A. C., stand for my parents' first names, Annie and Conrad. My dad, who loves to play poker, decided Ace was the perfect nickname for his son. My parents have a slightly warped sense of humor.

When I asked the Chief if he could share some information on a county resident, namely Mack Mills, I swear I saw a ghost pass in front of him. I put on my dad's poker face as I waited for a response. It never came. Instead, he just stared at me long enough to make me blink. I started to open my mouth, but decided to keep it shut. *Awkward.*

Finally he spoke, drawing out his words. "You. Are. Not. Going. To. Open. That. Can. Of. Worms. With. My. Help. Boy." Then he clammed up and stared down at his hands on top of the desk.

I thought I had entered the twilight zone and knew for certain this meeting was over. Before leaving I mumbled an apology for disturbing him. He didn't even look up or say goodbye when I left his office.

What in hell had caused that weird reaction from the Chief? My investigative nose was twitching and a headache was coming on. Better to deal with the headache first. A milkshake would give me the necessary brain freeze to recover from the shocking encounter so I headed for my therapy clinic, the Dairy Queen.

* * *

The four block walk gave me time to regroup. I pondered the last scene over and over in my head.

The Chief knew something, but the hot word was the name I had thrown on his desk. Who was Mack Mills? Why was the Chief protecting info on this dude? Could Mack Mills have crossed paths with his son Ben? Could there be a criminal record hidden away somewhere?

* * *

Slurping my milk shake, I walked back to the Post Gazette. My old metal desk is in the rear corner of the building with no window and terrible light. When I think, I twirl my pen and my chair at the same time. The seat has a tiny squeak, comforting, like a stuffed toy I slept with as a child. Suddenly a new idea on how to investigate the elusive Mack Mills came to me.

I headed back to the courthouse to check public records for title of ownership on anything owned by Mack Mills. After two hours and a lot of old ledgers, I found an LLC registered by two people with the county court clerk in 1955. One of them had the last name Mills, but his first name was Frank. The second name was Leon Cunningham. The name of the company was Frank's Fuel Oil. There was no phone number listed for the business and a P. O. box in Turtle Creek was the only address.

* * *

A quick trip to the Post Office confirmed a new owner for the box. Was this a lead or a dead end? I thought long and hard who else might be privy to information about elusive county residents and the name of an old friend came to mind. Time to turn over some rocks and find Cecil.

Chapter 4

The country hicks who flock to the Wal-Mart on Saturday also populate the county fair in the fall. Then they disappear to their caves for the rest of the year. Nobody in town knows where they live. Some clans home-school their brood, and undoubtedly teach hunting and fishing on a college level. Their driveways are dirt roads with a rusty mailbox or two announcing the entrance. Townies know better than to explore these roads alone. One way in and no way out. The Mills family might live far out in the boonies, but I didn't think they were red necks. Fortunately I know a professional hunter who is acquainted with the people who live at the end of dirt roads all over the county.

Cecil Martin has a high I.Q. with low ambitions. His goal in life is killing as many deer as possible. Gun or bow and arrow, didn't matter. With more deer than people in the county, he was happy, happy, happy all the time. I am convinced he is a reincarnation of Jeremiah Johnson. He went to college for two years, between hunting seasons, but hated every minute of it. He finally chose the woods and streams for his career and now leads hunting expeditions for white-collar city slickers. Knowing the hiding places of bail jumpers in the back woods gives him extra income as a bounty hunter for the county Sheriff. He makes enough money to get by and even owns a cell phone. I think most people who know him are in awe of his skills, but uncomfortable to be in the presence of a professional hunter.

His number was stored in my phone since I had called him several times for ideas to use in the hunting and fishing stories for the newspaper. He answered in his slow country drawl. "What can I do for you, Ace?"

"Need some information if you have it. You would be a confidential source for a story I'm working on. Interested?"

"Not yet, but I might be, if there's something in it for me. Tell me more," he said.

"How about I buy you lunch at Windy Hill Grill, say around two o'clock? I'll lay it all out after we eat."

He must have been hungry, because he was waiting in a rear booth when I arrived. The lunch crowd was gone, as I had hoped. No itchy ears to eavesdrop on our conversation. Wearing his usual daily attire, a full set of camouflage, including the hat that could not contain his flaming red hair which matched his handle-bar mustache. Why the deer did not see him from a mile away was a mystery.

The Grill was a greasy spoon kind of place. The fryers had probably never been allowed to cool off and the joint smelled heavenly. Cecil devoured the daily special platter of beer-battered catfish, hush-puppies, fries and coleslaw. After two giant-size glasses of sweet tea he was ready to listen and talk. He leaned back in the booth and patted his stomach. I had barely finished my burger and fries.

"You got my curiosity stirred up. What's this big secret meeting about, partner?"

I told him about the stalled six-year divorce marathon which I had witnessed in court and my interest in finding out more about the couple, Mack Mills and his wife, Ginny Faye.

He looked at me like I was from Mars. "Man, you don't know who the Mills family is?"

"I guess I'm too young to know everybody," I answered defensively. "And four years away at college left some information gaps. Can you tell me what you know about the family? All I could find was a business called Frank's Fuel Oil, owned by a Frank Mills, maybe a relative of Mack."

"Yeah, Mack's old man. Frank and his partner controlled the fuel oil market for decades, in at least three counties, and then Frank up and died. The partner, well I have no idea what happened to him, but he may be dead too. I think he had a son about the same age as Mack. Don't know how Mack got the business unless he bought out the partner's son, because later he told the stockholders he filed for bankruptcy, but that was a lie. Anyway, Mack turned around and sold the land for cash to an unknown party and pocketed the profits. Since he never filed bankruptcy, I suppose he committed fraud. I would love to know who fronted that money and why. All I know is Mack immediately built a truck stop on Interstate 40 and got rich doing it."

I guess the surprise showed on my face because he started to laugh. I wondered how he knew so much more than I did until I remembered how much higher his I.Q. was compared to mine. I found my tongue and shared my attempted interview with Chief Herring that went nowhere.

He said, "Oh brother, how little you know. Mack pissed off the stockholders when he claimed bankruptcy. One was George Herring, the police chief, who lost his share in the fuel oil business just when he needed to pay for Ben's college. I think that's why Ben joined the Marines. The Chief partially blamed the Mills family for Ben's death. I heard a lot of stuff when I baby-sat rich guys on hunting trips. Mack Mills had enemies out the wazoo."

I now understood why Chief Herring had a serious trust problem with Mack Mills and maybe even hated him. I probed some more. "Look, I know the partner's name was Leon Cunningham, but that's all I know. Have you heard of him or his son?"

"Nope, don't know any Cunninghams in this county," said Cecil, as he rose to leave. Leaning in close, he lowered his voice. "Watch your back, Ace. You're poking your nose in a dark cave and you don't know what's in there. These guys play for keeps."

"What do you mean?" I said.

"Remember some of those country boys we went to high school with? They couldn't ride the bus to school without somebody getting beat up. Now they're all grown up with guns."

He thanked me for the free lunch, stuck a toothpick in his mouth and stomped out of the restaurant in his waterproof boots, brandishing a big skinning knife on his belt.

The cheap vinyl booth felt cold as I sat there watching him leave. My feet had that numb, gone-to-sleep feeling but my brain was burning from the warning given by Cecil. I stayed where I was and thought about his other words of wisdom. *The only way to catch a snapping turtle without getting bit is to sneak up on his blind side and jerk his feet out from under him while he is floating along.* Sounded like a plan.

* * *

Finally, I slid out of the booth and stood up. My knees were shaky when I paid the tab. The walk down the hill into town did nothing to clear my head. I needed to get a second opinion from a clear-headed expert. At the bottom of the hill I took a right turn on East Main, walked one block and stopped in front of the Greyhound Auto Mart, my dad's used car business.

Conrad King was a mechanic in the military, then sold used cars for the Chevy dealership after he and my mom married, until the Ford dealership hired him as their sales manager. After I finished college, he felt free to become his own boss. When the city council voted to tear down the unused bus station, selling the concrete lot in the middle of town, he was the first in line to buy it. His mechanical background gave him a creditable advantage when he vouched for his used cars. Dad sold cars, Mom did the bookkeeping and I saved money toward my school loans by borrowing a car from the lot when I needed one. *Sweet.*

Chapter 5

Dad left work early on Wednesday, his poker night. He was on the phone when I popped in, and held up a finger for me to wait. I turned my back to give him some privacy and thought about how much to tell him. I had a nagging feeling that I might be getting in over my head by looking into a fraud scheme. He hung up the phone, locked the office door and we decided to walk home from the Greyhound Auto Mart with four blocks to talk. Dad did most of the listening.

"I met with a college friend today, Cecil Martin, and asked him what he knew about an old business formerly owned by two guys, Frank Mills and his partner, Leon Cunningham. I'm working on a new story for the paper, but after hitting a stone wall, I reached out for help. Cecil said that Frank's son, Mack, committed fraud after he inherited the business by telling the stockholders that he had to file for bankruptcy, but Cecil also said the filing never happened. Instead, Mack sold the land where the business was located for cash, keeping all the money for himself. The other owner, Leon and his son, are still a mystery."

Without stopping or turning to look at me, Dad said, "Okay, Ace. But why are you telling me and what do you want me to do?"

"Let's start with Chief Herring. According to Cecil, he was one of many who lost his investment money after Mack got his hands on the business. I tried to ask the Chief about Mack Mills, but he got very upset and refused to talk. You two go way back and play poker together. Can you find out more about that business and why Chief Herring and others thought it was a good idea?"

"This info you got from Cecil Martin; why the hell would he tell you what he did? Could it just be a rumor?"

"I like Cecil and we were friends in college. He is a very unusual person, but I trust and respect him. He has always had my back," I said.

"Tell me how you got involved in this," said Dad.

I filled him in on the divorce marathon and my hunch about a hidden back story steering me to investigate. By the time Dad and I arrived at the front door of our house, he had promised to sleuth around at the poker game tonight. We decided to leave Mom out of the loop until later. The wonderful smells of fried chicken and apple pie greeted us when we opened the door.

* * *

After dinner Dad went to his poker game down the street and Mom got a ride to Wednesday night bible study leaving me home alone. I fell asleep on the couch while watching CNN and woke up the next morning sporting a comforter that someone had tossed on me. I smelled bacon cooking and made a run for the shower. My parents had serious faces on at breakfast so I played along, drank my coffee and waited. But they surprised me.

Dad spoke first. "I had an interesting discussion with all the guys last night about the pros and cons of fuel oil vs. electricity. It made George Herring so uncomfortable that he left the game early. I also learned a lot about the economy after World War II. Fuel oil was liquid gold until the Tennessee Valley Authority started building the power plants on the Tennessee River in the fifties. TVA was supposed to provide cheap electricity to the southern states, but it took years to install the power lines to the country people who were in no hurry to wire their houses. They were content buying oil from Frank Mills and slow to switch over to electric.

"That's right," said Mom. "The ladies in my bible class had plenty to say."

So much for leaving Mom out of it.

She continued. "Some of my friend's husbands invested in Frank's Fuel Oil and were left with nothing when it closed. They knew Frank's son inherited the business after Frank died, but were surprised when Mack claimed bankruptcy. They assumed Frank had neglected the business before he died. No one guessed Mack had actually sold the business and walked away with the stockholders' money. Do you have any ideas, Ace?"

"Yep," I said. I suspected Ginny Faye Mills was holding the key to where the money trail led and knew much more than Cecil had told me. I could not wait to go back to the courthouse to observe the next hearing of Mills vs. Mills and was planning to arrange an interview with her as soon as the divorce was final.

Chapter 6

The next hearing for the Mill's pending divorce was coming up fast. I had done my homework by gleaning information from public records of the previous hearings. It was no secret that huge lawyer fees had been racked up after six years of unresolved litigation. After the third year, because the parties involved could not agree on anything, Judge Lester assigned Master Judge Harold Bell to arbitrate the division of assets and property. Judge Bell spent four days in private hearings with Ginny Faye Mills, Mack Mills, and their attorneys trying to hash it out. Only lawyers could present proof of assets to the court on behalf of their clients, which included six file boxes of financial information not available to the public. Judge Bell had spent two years sifting the contents of those boxes, after the four days of private hearings were over. He finally delivered his written opinion on the division of assets to Judge Lester's court.

Mack insisted, every chance he got, that he would delay the divorce for the rest of his life before he would give one penny to his estranged wife. Fortunately the court had awarded her spousal support at the beginning of the divorce hearings, which was all she had to live on. I would bet the court would never know the extent of all the investments Mack Mills had made with his untold fortune.

* * *

I stayed busy reporting and photographing various events to pacify my editor while anxiously awaiting the next scheduled hearing in a week. A county resident had killed a seven foot rattlesnake and called to get his picture in the paper. He had to stand on a step-stool in order to hold it up full length for the photo shot. He planned to cook the awesome thing for dinner that night. I hate snakes, dead or alive.

There is never an end to the weddings, sports events, civic meetings, award presentations, criminal activities and car accidents to report for the front page news. Part-time volunteers write the fluff-stuff : gossip columns, obituaries, home-style recipes and the classified section. Ads for revenue are sold by the editor's husband, James, a retired auctioneer. He and Loretta are both laid back employers. The Post Gazette is distributed to seventy-five percent of the county addresses once a week and local businesses pay generously to advertise for that much exposure. Although my job is secure, the pay is pathetic.

* * *

Time was passing slower than molasses until I researched the second owner on the LL C, Leon Cunningham. Who was he? There was no Leon Cunningham listed in the phone directory serving Fairfax County and Turtle Creek. Cecil had said he didn't know any Cunninghams. Mom inadvertently solved the mystery. She volunteers at the nursing home once a week and noticed the name, Leon Cunningham, from a list of patients posted at the front desk. I decided to pay a visit in person the next day. What I found was sobering with no possibility of an interview.

He resided in the advanced Alzheimer's wing, bedridden and curled on his side in a half ball, mouth open and snoring. The floor nurse who walked me to his room assumed I was a relative until I backed out and admitted I was a reporter. Unhappy, she pursed her lips together and shook her head as we left the smell of Pine Sol behind in the locked wing. I stopped again at the visitors desk on my way out, flashed my best smile for the pretty receptionist and asked, "Does Mr. Cunningham have any regular visitors?"

"His son, Kyle Cunningham visits every weekend from Jackson, Tennessee," she volunteered.

Have I just lucked up and located the other son?

I knew better than to ask for his address, but I did. She politely refused. I thanked her for nothing by blowing an air kiss as I turned to leave. She blushed.

* * *

With a borrowed car from Dad's lot, I hightailed it to Jackson that afternoon to track down Leon Cunningham's son, Kyle. His name was not listed in the phone book. I decided to inquire by way of the local police department, a method used to locate people who are hard to find. Of course they knew him.

One of the officers gave me a sly smile and said, "You can find him on Interstate 40, somewhere between Jackson and Memphis, if you drive ninety miles an hour until he pulls you over." The lame joke was enough to get a laugh from his fellow officers. Kyle Cunningham was a Tennessee state trooper. Oh brother, I can really pick 'em. After they told me where to find him, I tucked my tail in and backed out of the police station, bowing to their laughter.

* * *

The Highway Patrol Headquarters was located off the Interstate near Jackson. The duty chief informed me that Kyle's shift would soon end and I was welcome to wait in my car. And wait and wait and wait. No one was coming or going in the parking lot. One hour later he was still a no-show.

Suddenly the car began vibrating from a big hand slapping my window and motioning for me to put it down. He must have been watching me after dispatch tipped him off. Diligent was the first way to describe the big guy. The second way to describe him was more memorable. His belt buckle was above my window. All I saw was girth in a uniform. I dared not open the car door for fear of slamming into his nuts.

"Get out of the car. Now! Put your hands on the hood. Are you stalking me on state property? I need to see a driver's license. Do you have any weapons or drugs?"

Fortunately he protected his nuts by stepping back from the door before I got out.

"No Sir," I said in the polite tone I use at home and wished I was there instead of here.

When he ordered me to turn around, I could see the whole package. Thick neck on a rock solid body, short gray hair cropped to the scalp, pale blue eyes that betrayed his commanding voice and frozen facial expression. He was at least six foot four and approximately three hundred pounds in a tight brown uniform and hat that gave me a flash back to the Smokey Bear posters. Wow! I was super impressed. He looked like the human recruit for the Transformers. I stuck out my hand and introduced myself but he countered with a stare that could freeze a charging rhino and kept his hand on his gun.

"Why are you driving a car with a dealer tag?" he said.

"I get that a lot since my dad owns a used car business in Turtle Creek."

He relaxed his rigid stance and curiosity replaced anger on his face.

"So what do you want to talk to me about?" he said.

I seized the moment, asked for an interview and paused for an answer. My request hung in the humid air like damp sheets and the tension was heavy.

Kyle cleared his throat and asked, "An interview concerning what?"

I was ready to state my business and hoped he would cooperate.

Chapter 7

State employees are given the opportunity to eat their lunches on concrete picnic tables and benches, provided by Parks and Recreation of Tennessee, under big spreading oak trees. Kyle motioned for me to sit there so I backed up to a bench and sat. He remained standing, shading me like a tall building as he crossed his massive arms with hands like baseball mitts. Lord knows, he was a big man.

I held up my hands in mock surrender and showed him a friendly face. "Please, just call me Ace." I explained my initials, A. C. on my driver's license and told him about my job at the Post Gazette.

"This story may sound strange to you and I don't know what's going on yet, but I need to explore the clues. Your father was in business with a family named Mills, who seem a bit shady to me. My mom volunteers at your father's nursing home and they directed me to you. So here I am."

Squinting his eyes at me he said, "Go on," encouraging me to continue.

"Mack Mills and his wife are getting a divorce. The nasty dispute has been ongoing for six years, so I looked into the oddity of the whole thing and tripped over some public information. I found an LL C company, Franks Fuel Oil, registered by two owners, Frank Mills, Mack's father, and your father, Leon Cunningham. The LL C appears to have dissolved into bankruptcy but I think you might differ on that subject. So do you?"

"You're damn well right I differ on that subject," he spat out. "Mack and I were expected to run the business together someday, but his father died suddenly of a heart attack and my father was in first stage dementia."

"Were you ever in business with Mr. Mills?" I said.

"No. When Frank Mills died I was still in the army, with four more years before retirement. Mack and I didn't want to run the failing business so when he offered to buy out my half I jumped at it. Dad had given me power-of-attorney as soon as he was diagnosed. Mack paid me a paltry sum which seemed fair at the time and that money went for dad's care. That old business meant nothing to me."

"Do you have any clues what Mack did with the property after he bought you out?"

"Yes. There were rumors that Mack made a cash deal under the table, maybe with the Mafia after he settled with me. I also heard that he got rid of the stockholders by claiming bankruptcy. Someone bought that sorry piece of land with the underground tanks for God only knows what reason. I would bet those tanks have never been drained and the EPA would shit if they found out," said Kyle.

"Then why not turn 'em in or is there another missing piece of the puzzle?"

"I have been tempted to blow the whistle, but not until Dad passes away. Mack Mills is a vindictive SOB and revenge is his middle name. I'm glad Ginny Faye is divorcing him. You should definitely talk to her if you get a chance."

I don't think Kyle Cunningham took two breaths during that revealing confession. A powerful story was developing that needed to be proved, which was going to open the can of worms that Chief Herring wanted to keep the lid on. Cecil's admonition to be careful came back with a rush, but I did not share that with Kyle. I thanked him for his time and wished his father peace with his illness. He nodded and walked away. I got in my car and drove out of the lot. My thoughts were filled with questions I could not answer on the drive back to Turtle Creek. *Mafia? In Middle Tennessee? What could be their angle? How in the hell will I track this lead down?* Think, Ace, think. *What would anyone want with a polluted piece of land? Where is it anyway? Who knows how to find the property?*

My mind was racing and apparently so was I because flashing lights were on my tail. It was the Transformer himself, but not to give me a ticket.

When I lowered my window he stuck a rolled up piece of paper in my face.

"This is my private number. You are going to have a lot of questions later and I would rather you ask me before you ask the wrong person. I don't want to be responsible for your untimely death. Check out a faded billboard sign that says; Spa/Massages/Truckers Welcome. It's a few miles farther down on your right. The phone number on the sign has been disconnected. You get it all figured out and call me for more details. Okay?" I took his cell number and nodded an affirmative. Then he transformed back into a state trooper, did a U-turn across the median and drove off toward Jackson. I wondered what he was alluding to and why he was not telling me straight out.

* * *

As promised, the old billboard on stilts, erected on the edge of a cornfield in the middle of nowhere, loomed in my sight, followed by the backside of the billboard appearing in my right side mirror after I whizzed past. Did Ginny Faye know about the advertisement promising services for truckers? Was Kyle protecting someone by urging me to keep looking for a back story? I was starting to like this guy. All I could do was hope to interview Ginny Faye, after her next hearing which hopefully would be the final showdown ending the six year odyssey.

Chapter 8

Arriving early, I chose to sit in the front row of the courtroom for this hearing, instead of slouched in the back row, like the first time. My backpack was stuffed with legal pads, a cell phone, tape recorder and my laptop. No cameras were allowed in the courthouse and cell phones had to be off or in vibrate mode. I made my nest while watching the courthouse groupies straggle in and try to get comfortable on the bare wooden benches. Finally, the "all rise" command resounded from the bailiff. Judge Royce Lester II, without looking at anyone, made his way from his chambers to the bench carrying a thick binder. Another Mills vs. Mills hearing was about to begin and I wanted it to be the last.

With his combed-over, thin gray hair, freckles and wire rim glasses, Judge Lester reminded me of Mr. Magoo. Everyone knew the judge was poised to retire while he was still kicking ass. Thirty years of seeing only the worst in people had taken a toll. As soon as he put the offenders away, they made bail and were free to sin again. The ones who got no bail kept the county jail over-crowded while their trials dragged on, until most of them ended up in the Tennessee State Prison. Although Judge Lester appeared strict to the offenders, fairness was his true mantra. I admired the man after three years of observing his courtroom style.

All the main characters were present today for the umpteenth hearing. Failing a drum roll, I waited for the curtain to go up and the show to begin. The room was respectively quiet as Judge Lester sat down and began to shuffle his papers, like the maestro of his orchestra tuning up. He looked over his audience, waved his gavel high above his head, then dropped it loudly on the podium. Several people, including me, jumped in our seats and I knew something was different about this hearing from the last time.

With blustering fanfare, he immediately ordered counsel to stand up beside their clients, then proceeded to tell them that he intended to do all the talking today, warning them not to interrupt. Properly disciplined, they were mute as they sat down. Judge Lester cleared his throat and the oration began. I intended to record every word.

"I have reviewed this case many times over the past six years, but to continue these hearings any longer will make me physically ill. I believe, Mr. Mills, you could have settled this long ago, but you are consumed with greed and revenge and arrogance beyond description. Unfortunately, your character traits are not criminal or I would likely imprison you and throw away the key."

Mack Mills visibly flinched as he shifted in his seat. No one else moved a muscle. The Judge took no pause. "I don't blame Mrs. Mills for any of this mess created by you and your paramour. Collateral damage from this six year war will eventually backfire on you. Your misery, Mr. Mills, is just beginning as long as you believe the world revolves around you."

Before continuing, Judge Lester took a deep breath and a drink of water. "Furthermore, I am in complete agreement with Master Judge Harold Bell on the division of assets. I have reviewed his recommendations for the last time and that includes alimony payments, which I also intend to rule on today. Hear this Mr. Mills. You will pay all of Mrs. Mills remaining lawyer fees, as well as your own fees and any court costs as noted in the court reporter's records."

"Objection!" shouted Phyllis Faulker, rising from her seat.

The Judge pounded the podium and then pointed the gavel at her.

"You cannot object when I am speaking. I have listened to your objections for six long years and we are done," said Judge Lester. "Now please sit down and be quiet."

"But your honor, I will have to work for the rest of my life if you award her alimony," Mack said, defiantly standing up to face off with the judge. "And her lawyer fees have to be $100,000 at least. I can't afford to pay all that."

Staring directly at Mack, his face red and angry, Judge Lester raised his voice. "SIT DOWN! Do not interrupt me again. Your lawyer warned you about playing hard ball with me and you should have thought that through while you were delaying this divorce and accumulating huge fees. I suspect you have more assets than the audit uncovered and furthermore I believe Mrs. Mills deserves everything that she and her lawyer have asked for. She has been patient and polite in my courtroom and grossly distressed by your lack of cooperation. Losing her home, marriage and support because of your actions leaves me no choice. I intend to relieve her of some of the misery you rained down on her life."

"DO YOU UNDERSTAND ME, MR. MILLS?"

"There will be no merit in changing anything that you and your lawyer intended to contest today since this is the last hearing," said Judge Lester.

I wanted to applaud, but he was not finished.

"You are hereby ordered, Mr. Mills, by this court, to turn over her share of the truck stop business in the amount of the Master Judge's ruling of $500,000."

A collective gasp was heard in the courtroom.

"You have ninety days to produce the money or offer an acceptable payment plan to this court or you will be held in contempt, at which time I will gladly confine you to our fine local jail."

A huge groan escaped Mack Mills as he slumped in his seat.

Judge Lester turned to Ginny Faye Mills and his eyes softened a bit.

"Mrs. Mills, I grant you a divorce at this time and I hope happier days are soon to come."

Judge Lester then turned his attention to Phyllis Faulkner, Mack's attorney. "This court orders you to turn over to Mrs. Mills' attorney, the honorable Richard Pruett, all titles, deeds and other accounts set forth in the Master Judge's recommendation, within thirty days of this final hearing. That includes alimony payments which are to commence on the first day of next month. No excuses or appeals will be considered. This hearing is over."

Judge Lester pounded the podium, announced a one hour lunch break and dismissed the court until his afternoon session. Smiling, he left the room for his chambers. I was smiling too.

Not so for the incorrigible Mack Mills and his attorney.

They had a heartburn look of disbelief on their faces. Previous confidence was oozing away, as they sat in their seats as if in shock. Suddenly Mack stood up, shoving the table and soundly kicking his chair across the room. A barrage of cuss words spewed out. By the time the bailiff approached, the tantrum was over, calmed down by Phyllis Faulkner, who quickly gathered her files. Tugging Mack's coat sleeve, they exited the courthouse via the side door, avoiding the crowd at the front entrance that Ginny Faye and her lawyer had used. I had just seen a glimpse into the soul of a twisted man, with his true character on public display, and it disgusted me. I felt sorry for his attorney as well as his ex-wife.

* * *

Convinced that an interview with Ginny Faye was possible now that she was divorced, I followed her across Main Street to the law office of Richard Pruitt. The secretary offered me a seat in reception while they were meeting privately in the conference room. When they emerged and were done with hugs and handshakes, I stood to introduce myself. Mr. Pruitt vouched for me, which endeared him to me and no doubt got me the interview. If I ever needed a lawyer, he would be the man. Ginny Faye graciously agreed to meet with me at her home in Jackson for the interview and we exchanged contact information.

* * *

Anticipation washed over me as I practically ran to the Post Gazette to tell my editor the news. Since the two weeks had expired that Loretta had given me to investigate this story, now was the time to share my research with her. I hoped she would extend my assignment, once she heard about the purported fraud scheme. I told her about my interviews with Cecil Martin, outdoors man extraordinaire, and Kyle Cunningham, aka the Transformer. She asked if Chief Herring was helpful, so I answered that he was not, leaving out his negative reaction. I promised her a bigger piece of the puzzle after I met with Ginny Faye Mills.

Loretta scooted to the edge of her chair, elbows on the desk and a scowl on her brow, but she was hooked. There was a twinkle in her eyes and a half smile at the corner of her mouth.

"Sounds more like the beginning of a novel than a newspaper story," she teased.

"Now Loretta, you know I don't have time to write a novel with this all consuming job. I need to solve at least one mystery first."

I suspected she realized I would eventually leave for greener pastures, but not today. A juicy story was what her paper needed and this story was ripe for picking. Of course, she would keep her husband, James, informed knowing that he would love all the hullabaloo. She explained her main concerns for me; tread lightly and keep her up-to-date.

"Okay, Ace. Go do your thing and bring me a hell of a story when you finish solving this mystery." And with a flick of her wrist, I was dismissed by my boss.

Chapter 9

Ginny Faye suggested the following Sunday afternoon to meet at her home. I had rehearsed my questions on the drive to Jackson, but knew the interview would be a fishing trip. I hoped she would feel free to talk. Ringing the doorbell, I wondered if she was up for a grueling interview about her former husband.

A younger version of Ginny Faye opened the door and introduced herself as Sandra French, Ginny Faye's daughter. She appeared to be about my age, twenty five, and not wearing a wedding ring. Sandra offered me a seat on an expensive looking white leather sofa. The house was a small rental and the large furniture, from another lifestyle, looked misplaced. But somehow it all worked. Ginny Faye entered the living room carrying a tray of cookies and sweet tea intended for the coffee table. While I was encouraged to nibble goodies and sip the southern nectar we made polite talk.

She asked, "Why do you need to hear my story and what do you really want?"

I played the honest card. Ginny Faye was too nice to dance around so I jumped right to the point. "I want to know how your husband came into so much money and what he did with it," I blurted out, along with a few cookie crumbs.

Her laughter disarmed me. "How much time do you have Mr. King? This story could on all afternoon."

Stunned into believing that I had hit the mother lode, I lost my tongue temporarily. Pushing my recorder across the coffee table and turning it on, I felt destined to discover part of this mystery today. I was giddy with anticipation and determined to hang on to every word.

"Ah, the money," Ginny Faye began. "Mack could never get enough; even stole from his mother after his father died. He reasoned that her money was his birth right and thought his mother was too stupid to handle spare change."

"Does Mack live with his mother or is she living alone?" I asked.

Shaking her head, she explained, "No, Mack lives with a woman in Turtle Creek. His mother is still in the farmhouse at eighty with a full-time companion. Mack rarely visits his mother to avoid her constant meddling. He was their only child and spoiled rotten by both parents. He can be very charismatic toward anyone he intends to exploit."

"How did he exploit you?"

"Mack wanted a wife he could manipulate and control. He picked the poorest little church mouse he could find. Me. I was naive and ignorant when we made our bed together. All he wanted was a dependent wife who made him look good, didn't talk back and was loyal, like a dog. I could never please him or his mother no matter how much I tried. Mack is self-centered, delusional and a pathological liar. Those are just a few of his short comings," said Ginny Faye.

I wondered what Sandra thought about the trashing Mack was getting. Feeling uncomfortable, I shifted my position on the sofa, and stole a glance in her direction. Sandra was smiling. The two women must have read my mind because Ginny Faye stated a new fact to me.

"Mack and I have no children together. My first husband, Sandra's father, is long gone, maybe even dead. Do you object to my daughter listening in on our interview?"

I looked from Ginny Faye to Sandra and answered, "Not at all. Please continue."

"Our business was not just a means to an end for Mack. He saw dollar signs on anything he touched and wanted more. Greed and acquisition is a driving force in his mind that he relates to success," said Ginny Faye.

"Are you referring to the truck stop?" I asked.

"Yes, but Mack owned a roadhouse cafe before our first truck stop. I was managing a restaurant when we met and he needed a cook. I worked for years as an unpaid employee after we married, accumulating no benefits. Mack paid me with a lavish lifestyle: big house, ski trips, cruises and fancy cars, to name a few. But that is not the reason we got divorced. He never thought he would get caught cheating. When he did get caught he mocked me with his arrogance."

"How did he do that?"

"Mack told me that I could not make it without his money and would never leave him. He saw me as personal property, like chattel. When I moved out, he bragged that I would eventually fold, grovel to come back and never go through with the divorce. He was so full of himself, wanting to have a wife and keep a mistress on the side. I had no choice but to file for divorce." Ginny Faye paused as if she still could not believe it.

"That was Mack's first reality shock, underestimating me. He had refused my reasonable offers to settle over and over, dragging out the hearings for six years. The delayed time did not work in his favor, but allowed me the time to grow some backbone. His second reality shock came during the discovery hearings when he realized I knew more than he thought about his business deals. He dug his heels in deeper to keep 'his' money as long as he could."

"About those business deals; what really happened to his father's fuel oil business? I heard rumors that Mack filed for bankruptcy, cutting out the stockholders, but then sold the land privately for cash in a shady deal, pocketing the money for himself."

"You are correct. It was out and out fraud. He threw the stockholders to the wolves," said Ginny Faye.

"Can you give me your impressions of the former oil business or memories regarding location?" I asked. "I would like to investigate the property personally."

"Let me think about that. I remember the business was isolated out in the country, between the Fox River and the Tennessee River. The partners, Frank and Leon, co-owned a few trucks and some tanks located underground for the oil. A chain link fence surrounded the perimeter to keep trespassers out. I also remember a construction trailer on the property that was used as an office. Mack sold the trucks along with the trailer after his father died. I know because I saw a bill of sale for that equipment during tax season one year. Perhaps the chain link fence is still standing. I only saw the place once while we were married. I was not impressed," she said.

"Do you remember hearing anything about how or where the oil got delivered to the property from river barges?"

"No, but Tom Warren lives on the Fox River and fished and hunted up and down the Tennessee River all his life. He may know how to get to the property. He and Mack grew up on farms next to each other, but were never friends. Got into fights at school all the time. Later they had a huge falling out over a woman and payback might appeal to Tom. I know it sounds like a long shot but then we can't exactly ask Mack where it is, can we?" stated Ginny Faye sarcastically.

"Do you remember if the business had telephone lines to the property?"

"Yes. They had to take orders from customers to deliver the oil. The partners, Frank and Leon, were on the site several hours each day to take calls. They took turns making deliveries the rest of the day. Why are you so interested in that old business?" said Ginny Faye, a perplexed frown on her brow.

Shrugging, I responded, "That's not important to me. I want to know who in their right mind would buy a scraggly piece of undeveloped land, for cash, and how they planned to use it."

Sandra spoke up for the first time, "Maybe someone who has something to hide, don't you think?"

As if on cue, we all bobbled our heads. I asked the next question.

"Wonder why so many people bought stock in Frank's Fuel Oil and risked their hard earned money?"

"Because fuel oil ruled before TVA," explained Ginny Faye. "Everyone believed that electricity would cost a lot more than fuel oil to heat their homes, not to mention taking years to get poles and lines in place deep within the county. Remember, back then those old farm houses were not wired for electricity. Frank's Fuel Oil wanted to keep going and did not believe their customers would ever cross over to electric heat. Frank and Leon were living in the past when they decided to sell stock options that never paid a dime. Mack convinced the stockholders that his father's poor choices had been the kiss of death for any future profits, leaving him no choice but to file bankruptcy. He also told the stockholders that the land was worthless with four oil tanks buried underground. They bought the story and Mack sold the land for cash, pocketing the money for his own gains."

"I'm assuming the cash was used for the truck stop. Right?" I asked.

"No. The cash was used as a down payment for our first and smallest truck stop, enough to qualify Mack for a commercial loan. Three years later it burned to the ground."

"What? Wait a minute. You and Mack owned two different truck stops?" I asked.

"Yes, I assumed you knew that. Sorry if I didn't make myself clear. The cash from the land deal made it possible to build the first truck stop, the one that burned. When Mack's fire insurance came up short, he tried to find commercial bankers to back a rebuild. They turned him down

as high risk because of the fire. He didn't know
where to turn, until the same people who bought
the land with cash, came forward again with cash
to invest. All of a sudden enough money was
available to build a second and much bigger truck
stop. Mack was puffed up with pride, giving
himself accolades for his brilliant maneuver. He
never knew he had made a deal with the devil,"
she said.

"How did Mack manage to fool the
stockholders regarding the bankruptcy fraud?"

"Like most gentlemen in the south, they
blindly trusted Mack's word. Gullible? Yes, but a
handshake meant something. Mack counted on
being able to pull the wool over their eyes and it
worked. Of course, after that they lost trust in him,
but he didn't give a flip. He had bigger fish to fry
and new money in his pocket."

When a reporter is doing an interview, he
knows when to abruptly change the subject with
a surprise question. Now was the time to shake
things up and see what poured out.

"What do you know about an old billboard
on the interstate with a defunct phone number
advertising services for truckers?"

Ginny Faye's eyes widened in surprise. "How
in the world did you find out about that?"

"From a highway patrolman named Kyle
Cunningham," I replied.

"Do you mean Leon Cunningham's son? Well Ace, you are just full of surprises. How did you connect those dots?"

"It's a long story, but believe me he has no love for your ex-husband."

Ginny Faye leaned back, drew in a long breath and glanced at her daughter before she exhaled and spoke again.

"Well, here's the rest of the story. The questionable all-cash loan for the second truck stop came with strings attached. One of the conditions in the contract was to include a motel for the truckers when the new and bigger truck stop was built. Mack's paramour, who used to be our bookkeeper, is now the 'madam' of that motel, overseeing the truckers' needs. She and Mack are running a whore house hidden in the truck stop.

The story was peeling like an onion right before my eyes. The more I found out the more I wanted to 'cry uncle'. *What the hell have I gotten myself into?* Morbid curiosity quickly overcame my concern. I was not scared enough to walk away from this fascinating story. Had the living room suddenly gotten warmer?

My next question was predictable. "Who is this madam?"

"Josie Cagle. She was once a trusted friend," said Ginny Faye.

"Not - mom's - friend - anymore," added Sandra.

"Perfectly understandable. Let's move on. Why do you think this guy, Tom Warren can help?

This was answered by Sandra. "Tom and his brothers inherited a 300 acre farm when their parents died. Their rich bottom land fronted the Fox River next door to the Mill's property. Tom's brothers wanted nothing to do with farming so Tom bought them out. After working his way through a degree at the University of Tennessee, he bought a pedigree Black Angus bull and became a success story in a dying profession."

"What happened between Tom and Mack that caused such a riff?" I asked.

Ginny Faye continued the story. "There were bad feelings between Tom and Mack since they were boys. Remember, Mack was an only child and never learned how to share. Tom's young wife, beautiful, but stupid, had a brief torrid affair with Mack. The betrayal enraged Tom. He divorced her and never married again. The hapless affair occurred long ago, before I met Mack, but the hate is still simmering between those two."

My recorder gave two warning beeps before the batteries died. I couldn't believe how forgetful I was not to bring backups. Sadly, this interview was over, for now. Leaving was hard with so many unanswered questions filling my head. They invited me back again and waved good-by from the front porch.

* * *

As I drove back to Turtle Creek, I mentally sifted through the amazing amount of information. Before asking Tom Warren for help in finding the elusive property, I would listen to this tape again to get the facts sorted out. If the mafia had loaned Mack money for the second truck stop including a whore house, then they probably bought the land where the oil business once stood. But why? If Mack was stuck in the middle with crime squeezing in from all sides, he was in a world of trouble. Also, how did Josie Cagle go from being Mack's bookkeeper to the madam for his whorehouse? As the Judge said to Mack Mills, "what a mess you have created". I could visualize my grandmother shaking her head and saying, "There ain't no rhyme nor reason to what some people say and do."

All this speculation was getting me no answers. I drove past the beckoning billboard sign advertising those shady services with a disconnected phone number. Another piece of the puzzle snapped together. The rotting sign promoted a prior location. The current truck stop was a different animal. Kyle Cunningham owed me those 'details' he had hinted about and I planned to ask him what they were.

I could understand the mafia and prostitution all wrapped up together, but the purchase of the deserted piece of property looked like an unconnected event. More proof was needed that the mafia was involved in this collusion. Who were they and why was their interest so far removed from Memphis? Maybe I should look outside the box and just work one angle at a time.

Chapter 10

First things first. I would call Tom Warren. If he agreed to an exploratory visit on his farm, then my second call would be to Cecil Martin. I needed a guide to Tom's property. Kyle Cunningham moved to number three. No less important, just business.

As soon as I got back to Turtle Creek, I called Tom. After an introduction, I explained that I wanted to expose the dirty business deals of Mack Mills and what I was looking for. Tom confirmed that a defunct bridge spanning the Fox River at the north end of his property connected to a road which led to the site. He generously offered to lead me and Cecil to the cross point. He gave no guarantees about the bridge's dilapidated condition and claimed that he had not used it for years. We set a date to meet at his house and check out the possibility of a way to the property.

Later, when I searched Google Earth, the bridge and cross road were not to be seen from space. Many dirt roads running north and south were cut off with no exits in the 1950's after the debut of Interstate 40, which traverses east and west across Tennessee. I should have suspected a problem but ignored the computer's wisdom.

Cecil was all in when I called and asked for his help to locate the property. He was confident that we could walk across the one-lane bridge used by traffic years ago. I agreed to the sensible approach instead of wading the river and risking possible drowning by stepping in a deep hole. The plan was for Tom to wait in his truck on his side of the river while we explored the far side, assuming we could cross the bridge. This mission should be the easiest way to find the route leading to the site of the lost oil business. What could go wrong?

* * *

With a borrowed car from dad's lot, I picked up Cecil in front of the county jail early the next morning as a light rain began to fall in Fairfax County. Tom's farm was far out in the sticks and I was lost after two turn-offs on unimproved roads. Cecil gave me directions and navigated the winding roads like an Indian guide. The wind buffeted our small car and the rain became heavier as we drove farther into farm country. Black Angus cattle appeared unfazed by the downpour and grazed on without looking up.

On our arrival, Tom's mongrel dog barked, but had sense enough to stay under the porch while we covered ourselves with cheap plastic rain covers, provided by Tom. After piling into Tom's F-350 truck with oversized mud tires, we moon-bounced across a cow pasture and parked about fifty yards from the bridge. We proceeded to walk single file in the rain with Tom leading. I thought we looked ridiculous in our yellow parkas, like Huey, Dewey and Louie on a field trip.

The rain had not slacked off and after a sloppy walk through muck and dodging cow-pies, we stood before the one-lane bridge. No one said a word as we stared at the ominous sight before us. Veiled by the rain on my glasses, like a vision through a seeded glass window, the once-painted steel framework had morphed into a rusting pile of metal. The bridge was covered in kudzu vines which can grow up to a foot a day nine months out of the year. Mother Nature's attempt to comfort the sagging, lonely structure. No wonder the incognito bridge didn't show up on Google. Like an abandoned orphan, there was no name plate on its frame, but Tom said it was called the prison bridge because of the proximity to the Tennessee State Prison. The overgrowth of kudzu that imprisoned the bridge had sentenced it to a sad and hopeless future.

Cecil stepped out, testing the first board and the sleeping giant awakened with moans and creaks and cracking sounds. After giving the problem some thought, he wisely decided we should distribute our weight by crossing one at a time. Because I weighed less than he did, the short straw went to me to cross first. Reluctantly, I started feeling my way, slowly side-stepping across with a sliding motion until I was near the middle of the bridge. Leaves and small branches covered the wooden running boards. So far, so good. I turned, stopped and gave Cecil the thumbs up sign.

As soon as Cecil stepped on the bridge, I fell through. The center just collapsed with a loud implosion of falling wood, dirt, leaves and me. I let out a blood-curdling yell, expecting to hit hard in the shallow rocky bed, but my body bounced up and down like I was attached to a bungee-cord. The thick kudzu vines had ensnared me in mid-air and maybe saved my life. I was suspended hanging upside down by one leg over the river. I knew now how a fly feels when it hits a spider web. The entire bridge sounded like it wanted to collapse with me, squeaking and moaning above me. Then it was dead quiet. Just when I thought things could not get any worse, they did.

Not more than ten feet from my face, at the edge of the river bank, was a seething pile of agitated cottonmouths. Their nest had no doubt been disturbed by the falling debris. I hate snakes. And cottonmouths are poisonous. I screamed like a girl, "Help, Help!"

Cecil yelled, "I'm coming Ace." He was already on his way down the bank, but Tom beat him to me.

"Stand back," he yelled to Cecil. He began mowing the slimy reptiles down as they crawled all over each other to get away. Thank God, Tom had brought a pistol loaded with snake shot. My heart was beating furiously and although only a few minutes had passed it seemed much longer before my heroes untangled and cut the vines enough to lower me down. With my arms over their shoulders for support, we trudged up the bank and out of the shallow river bed as fast as possible. By the time we got in the truck, we were chilled to the bone.

The bumpy drive back to Tom's house was drippy. No one was talking but our sense of disappointment filled the truck cab. I thought I heard Tom's dog laughing under the porch when we waddled up the front steps to shed our duck disguises. We stood in front of Tom's gas fireplace to dry out and regain our dignity. Maybe we should dynamite the old bridge to kingdom come if Cecil and I are ever invited back. Not likely.

Chapter 11

After the heart-stopping bridge fiasco, Cecil and I dealt with the experience in our own way as we drove back to Turtle Creek. I craved a fix from the Dairy Queen while Cecil was deep inside his big brain. I hoped he was percolating another idea on how to gain access to the oil business property. He was and he shared the idea.

"We could float down river to the spot where barges used to off-load the oil before the flood. You said that Ginny Faye told you about telephone lines to the business. We could look for any old poles still standing that veer off to nowhere and follow them to wherever," he said.

The hair-brained plan actually seemed logical to me coming from a genius. After we filled up on burgers and shakes, I dropped him off beside his pick-up truck at the county jail parking lot. I dared not show up at the Post Gazette looking like something a washing machine had spit out, and according to Cecil, I smelled like a river rat. It was only noon, but the day was over for me. I had no choice but to go home.

* * *

After washing away the mud and river smell in a hot shower, I made an assessment of my bruised body. The leg that got caught up in the kudzu vines was the worst. The hip joint had been on the verge of dislocation, but remained intact. Scratches from the falling bridge debris were superficial, but I had a black eye with no clue how that happened. Maybe the bridge resented being awakened. I crawled under the sheets and my last thought before sleep promised I would have a sore body tomorrow. Thankfully, Mom was at the nursing home and Dad was at work selling cars. I just needed a little nap.

* * *

Mom cracked my door to announce dinner was ready, having no idea I had been in bed all afternoon. Groggy and disoriented, I sat up and tried to swing my legs off the bed, but one leg refused to move sideways. When I tried to look at my legs, one of my eyes would not open. I checked the time on the bedside clock with one eye. Five hours had passed since I laid down for my little siesta. Then I remembered; almost falling into a snake pit. *What idiot would do what I had just done?*

Crawling out of the bed was no easier than standing upright. Taking that first step sent a wave of pain to my hip joint. Trying to put on clean briefs, with one leg barely working was hilarious, except for the pain. I ditched the underwear and settled for a pair of oversized running shorts, added a clean tee shirt and limped into the kitchen.

My parents took one look at me and asked the same question together.

"What happened to you?"

"I fell off a bridge. No, actually I fell through a bridge and almost got bit by cottonmouths. The kudzu vines snagged me just in time. I was hanging upside down over the river until Cecil and Tom rescued me after Tom shot the snakes. What's for dinner?"

Mouths were hanging open, horrified looks frozen on their faces.

"Ace, you look awful. Are you hurt? Who gave you that shiner?" said Dad.

"Why are you limping so bad?" said Mom, with concern on her face.

"I've stiffened up some since this morning, but I'll be all right in a day or two. I don't know how I got a black eye."

My Dad looked put out. "Yeah, maybe you'll be able to open your eye in a day or two. Have you looked in a mirror son, because I think a trip to the emergency room would be a good idea before we eat dinner."

"Now calm down Conrad. Let's see if Ace can sit down first. Dinner is getting cold, you know," said Mom.

"Don't tell me to calm down, Annie. What about my car? Does it look as bad as Ace?"

"Dad, the car is fine. We went to the river in Tom's truck so we wouldn't get stuck in the mud. You do know Tom Warren, the cattle rancher, don't you?"

"Don't know him, but I expect to hear the full story during dinner. Let's eat."

The truth did little to calm down my parents. They were clearly upset with my brush with death story. So was I, but they could not know how cautious I would be from now on. Staring snakes in the face sobers a man real fast.

* * *

Throwing my insurance card around the next day got me an X-ray for the hip and an eye exam by the local optometrist. A call to Loretta from the doctors office filled her in on part of the story before I showed up at the newspaper office. Nothing was permanently damaged, but I looked like a car wreck happened anyway.

I spent a lot of time thinking about where this mystery was leading. There was a lot more to be learned from Ginny Faye Mills and as soon as I could comfortably sit long enough to drive, I would go back to Jackson for another round of interviews with her. I wanted to talk to Kyle Cunningham again. I wanted to get the whole story about how the mafia got involved, hoping the three of us could sit down together. I started compiling a new list of questions and purchased a dozen batteries for my tape recorder in preparation for the next interview. Before setting up the interviews, I needed time to heal and take on some new projects at my job.

* * *

A major story was scheduled for next week's edition; the retirement celebration for Judge Royce Lester. Yes, he was finally going to do it; retire before he died in office. When Loretta assigned the coverage to me I was thrilled for two reasons: I admired the man's career and second, I coveted a private interview with him regarding the Mills divorce marathon once he was retired.

The cocktail party, arranged by his wife, was being held at their mansion this coming Sunday afternoon. There was one upscale subdivision in Turtle Creek and they owned the largest house there, a two-story white brick with six white columns spanning the front porch. The style was a throwback to southern plantations and appropriate for a sitting judge. Following a large catered party, the celebration would progress to the best restaurant in town, Golden Oaks, reserved for a sit down dinner with his closest friends and family.

The assignment was for me to write the lead story and take photos for the front page followed by another spread on the society page. My damaged eye was now working enough to use a camera and only a slight limp reminded me of my "Indiana Jones" adventure.

As a courtesy, I called the judge's wife to introduce myself. Ms. Sara Lester confirmed that she had mailed my invitation in care of The Post Gazette. When I asked if there would be any security, she seemed amused by the question.

"Just sign the guest book when you arrive at the front door, Ace. And please wear a suit and tie."

"I will and don't worry about the article or pictures. The paper will showcase the best coverage for you and your husband and that's a promise."

We hung up and I thought again about them not having any security. *I guess they don't expect any party crashers.*

Chapter 12

I dressed for the Sunday afternoon celebration in my only suit and a sunny yellow tie and felt pretty good when I looked in the mirror. In spite of my glasses, the yellow bruising around my eye still showed. Coordination is a talent.

The reception at the mansion started at five. I arrived early to check the lay-out and choose the best back-drop locations of the house and gardens for photos. A young girl, most likely a granddaughter, with missing teeth and long pigtails was stationed at the front door in charge of the guest book. She batted her eyes at each guest. What a sweetheart. After taking a couple of photos of her, I scanned the front room, checking out the people as they arrived.

With most of the men in tuxes, accompanied by ladies in beautiful dresses and jewels, the guests looked important. I posed and photographed many of them, aided by the soft light of a summer afternoon.

And then I saw her. Floating like a princess across the sun room, balancing a tray of canapés. I stood still and waited until Sandra French turned around. She recognized me and gave me a stunning smile.

"Ace, what are you doing here?" she asked.

"Reporting for the paper. And you?"

"Catering the party; part of my job at Golden Oaks. Would you take a picture of me with Judge Lester and his wife before I have to leave?"

"Yes, but why leave now?"

"The dinner at Golden Oaks. I've managed their kitchen since last year," she said. "Surprised?"

Disappointed you are leaving, I thought. "Nope, not surprised," I said.

* * *

Around seven, when the cocktail party was over, the dinner group of two dozen special guests moved to the restaurant. I followed them inside for last minute photos. Three big round tables had been reserved and roped off for eight people each, near the front of the main dining room. Each table was laden with elegant center pieces. The salads had just been served; my cue to leave, but fate interrupted.

A loud disturbance could be heard at the rear of the restaurant in the kitchen. The sounds of dishes being dropped and people yelling were occurring together. The double swinging doors from the kitchen flew open and all hell broke loose. A man dressed in black, wearing a ski mask and holding a sawed off shotgun burst onto the scene. He lowered to one knee, glancing at each table until he saw the one where Judge Lester was seated. When he racked the gun preparing to shoot, my camera was already raised with my finger on the flash button. I pressed it. His head jerked toward me. The flash had distracted him for a second or two.

Chief Herring's reaction was immediate and he drew his 357 Magnum. Never mind that he almost shot his foot off by discharging his weapon straight down prematurely, but the report from the big gun proved too much for the would-be assassin. He sprang up, bolted for the kitchen and headed for the rear door leading into the back alley.

Pure bedlam had broken out in the room even though the perp failed to fire his gun. Chief Herring took off in pursuit like a hound chasing a fox. The sound of more broken dishes and loud voices accompanied the retreat and ensuing chase. I was able to focus on the chaotic scene in the dining room and took a dozen photos of the guests reactions. They were all standing up, but no one ran for the front door. Mass confusion prevailed, but not everyone had seen what happened. The guests were asking questions, but a logical explanation would not be forthcoming any time soon. There was no logic to an attempted murder by a lone gunman, in a crowded restaurant on a Sunday night.

Somebody wanted the Judge dead and damn near pulled it off. Who and why?

After about three minutes, Chief Herring reappeared through the kitchen doors. Everyone was standing like the help, clenching their napkins and waiting for the shoe to drop before he spoke. The Chief was in a rage from the look on his red face.

"Missed him, damn it. He had a motorcycle stashed in the alley. Did any of you recognize him behind all that black?"

Some people muttered "no," shaking their heads as they looked around. Sara Lester started to cry. The Judge put his arm around her protectively. Several sat down amid the confusion. One guy started to eat his salad. They all followed his lead and slowly sat down and one by one picked up their fork. Judge Lester and Chief Herring both started talking at the same time, then stopped to regroup with nods to each other. The Judge would have used his gavel to restore order if it was available.

Instead, he cleared his throat and said, "Well, now that the entertainment is over, let's try and salvage this fine meal or what's left of it." He motioned for Sandra to approach and requested a report on the state of the kitchen.

"All the food is ready and we can serve if you like. Just a few broken dishes along with a pile of pots and pans, but no big mess to clean up. The special cake was not near the action, but maybe Ace should take a photo of it now in case the guy in black comes back." A few nervous laughs were heard.

Chief Herring had disappeared to order an APB from his cruiser. Sara Lester had stopped crying but everyone present was dumb-founded over the previous scene. This retirement dinner would be the talk of the town for months and not because of the delicious food.

* * *

True to form, Buzz's Barbershop was a bee hive the following morning. I showed up at eight for a trim and the joint was packed. The chairs were full and they were talking about the almost murder, but nobody knew nothing about it. They sounded like a gaggle of gossips just repeating the same questions. There were no answers.

I skipped the crowded barber shop, revealing nothing to the other patrons about the photos I had taken last night and headed directly for the police station. Everyone in the county would have the opportunity to see those pictures on the front page of the Gazette this week and the Nashville Tennessean paper. An image of the man in black, posturing to assassinate the Judge, was concealed in a white file folder under wraps with me. The investigation would be getting started this morning and I didn't want to be left out. I arrived at the police station at eight fifteen, full of vim and vigor.

Chapter 13

Chief Herring had been in his office since daybreak, like a general planning a siege on crime, according to his frazzled dispatcher. She was reeling from all the calls and E-mails. Interview requests were pouring in from cable TV, metropolitan newspapers and law enforcement agencies all over the state. Media outlets were mesmerized by the close brush with death of a well-known Judge.

The County Sheriff, Pat Garrett, had also showed up early. The two men had their backs to the glass door and heads together in conversation while looking at the floor. I waited politely for a chance to get in with the big boys and reveal my evidence. Five minutes went by, but after another five minutes I couldn't stand it any longer. They looked up in surprise when I crashed their meeting holding my file folder high in the air like a white flag.

"I got a picture of the bad guy you need to see," I loudly announced.

They almost fell over each other pulling up a chair up for one impatient reporter. The huddle became three with me in the center.

The dining room in the restaurant had been well lit, producing clear images in every photo including the most important one. They couldn't believe their eyes. The shooter was clearly Caucasian, presenting enough white skin around the openings of the ski mask. His height was harder to determine due to the kneeling position but weight appeared to be about 165. The shoes in the photo were not for hunting but desert boot style, ankle high and dark brown or black. Pants and hoodie were black like the mask, but the gloves were lighter, similar to deer skin. I thought the boots and gloves looked expensive compared to the rest of his clothes.

The Chief and Sheriff were fixated on the gun the assassin held and knew they were looking at a sawed off, 20-gauge, double barrel. I knew about snake shot but nothing else about guns. Sitting in a circle, we were intently studying the photo in total silence when the intercom interrupted to announce another visitor. Our concentration was put on hold as we all looked toward the glass door.

"Who is it?" bellowed Chief Herring to his dispatcher. She never got to answer.

Judge Lester charged through the door, like it was his office.

The Chief's chair fell over when he stood up, but he recovered quickly and offered the fallen chair to the Judge who waved it off. Standing before us with his hands on his hips and a chiseled face, he certainly had the floor.

"By God, I'm not retiring until this is settled even if it takes years. Whoever tried to shoot me will not get off on a technicality if I can help it. What do you know?"

"Calm yourself, Judge, and have a look at your enemy," said Chief Herring.

"Let me see the idiot."

The photo was handed to the Judge, passed around again and discussed at length, but no new clues came to light. The Judge admitted he had dozens of enemies, most of them locked away. He conceded the possibility that revenge could be arranged from behind bars, but no threats had been made, if that was the motive.

My cell phone vibrated, providing a good excuse to leave the room. Let the big boys handle it from now on. They had the photo and interviews to work with. I had a paper waiting to get printed. All three stood to shake my hand. A gracious tradition among Southern gentlemen.

* * *

My editor, Loretta was the caller and I told her about the photo. She was almost hyperventilating when I arrived at the office and showed her a copy. The paper would be a lot thicker this week with the picture of the mysterious man in black filling the front page. The story would jump

over to pages two and three with more photos of
the restaurant witnesses and their statements,
even though they had little to offer. No one had
any idea who tried to kill the Judge. With no leads
or developments, the incident would be boring
after a week and forgotten after two weeks.

* * *

I must have looked at that person in the photo
a hundred times in the ensuing days. A nagging
feeling never left me that more information lurked
below the surface and beyond my comprehension.

Pursuing Mack Mills and his shady businesses
had been on hold for too long and now that my
hip had healed, I geared up for another trip to
Jackson.

I called Ginny Faye and finagled a
continuance of the first interview with her. She
suggested we include Kyle Cunningham, which
caught me completely by surprise. That was
supposed to be my idea. She explained her
reasoning which was very enlightening.

"He knows the history of Mack's prostitution
business because he was there when the Tennessee
Bureau of Investigation raided the location. Plus,
I would love to see him again," she said.

That statement cleared up the mystery of
what Kyle knew about the old billboard
advertising services for truckers.. He was part of
that raid, but felt it was not his place to tell me.

Including Kyle in her next interview made perfect sense. She read my mind about combining their interviews and confirmed my hunch that she knew a lot more about her ex-husband's business deals.

I played along with her idea. "That might work if Kyle cooperates. I'll call him, see when he's free and call you back."

When I called Kyle, he only needed to know where and when. Ginny Faye had suggested the place and time; a little eatery in the Jackson Hotel on Sunday afternoon. We hung up on the same page. With a big smile, I did a fist pump, adding a resounding, "Yes!"

Chapter 14

We met at 3 o'clock in a room with a decimated buffet. The church goers had finished off the most recent 'last supper' and departed. The place was closing at four but offered the privacy we needed. An hour was plenty of time. Kyle hugged Ginny Faye like a long lost sister, crushed my hand in greeting and the interview formally began when I pulled out the recorder.

"Is that thing on?" said Kyle.

"Yes, is that a problem?" I said.

"Only if the mafia gets their hands on it."

"I can promise you this interview will be secure until it's safe to unwrap it."

Ginny Faye added, "You can count me in but I certainly don't want Mack to hear the things I'm exposing about him, especially if he's in cahoots with the same bad boys."

"Then we all agree," I said. "The exposure of criminal activities is scary stuff. We gotta be careful, and keep all shared information to ourselves. We can only take this to the DA when we have enough evidence to convince him there is a case. Both of you would be credible witnesses if we can pull this off. Are you ready to start talking?"

"Ginny, would you like to tell Ace how the prostitution got started in the first place?" said Kyle.

"Y'all humor me while I go back about ten years. Mack went on a business trip with a fly-by-night investment partner. I was not suspicious until they returned. He went on a little too much about the good times they had. Mack and his shady partner co-owned an old Shell station, broken down and inoperable when purchased. Their intention to do a remodel changed after their trip. Because the Shell station was on valuable property fronting an exit road on Interstate 40, they hatched a better idea. They purchased two double-wide trailers and positioned them behind the closed gas station. Mack claimed the rental income, generated by the two trailers, would more than pay the taxes on the land. He said they would always be booked by hunters and fisherman staying long weekends near the river. What a crock."

"How did you find out Mack was lying?" I said.

"A billboard on I-40, east of Jackson, went up right after the trailers were delivered. There was a duplicate billboard set up west of Nashville. I became curious, called the number on the billboard from a pay phone and immediately recognized Josie's voice, Mack's book keeper. I was flabbergasted and hung up instantly. It was obvious Josie was making the appointments when the truckers called."

"What reaction did you have to that revelation?"

"Needing absolute confirmation, I went to the trailers pretending to be the cleaning woman. An Asian girl answered the door, looked scared and said, "Busy now, come back." The girls had to be from Nashville, working part-time shifts in the trailers, which explains why Josie was running back and forth to Nashville every other night. She was flying blind and didn't know squat about running a whore house," said Ginny Faye.

"Why did the men take such a chance putting up those two billboards?" I asked.

"Mack and his partner were making a lot of money with very little overhead. The customers could park their big rigs in front of the defunct gas station and walk to the trailers for service. People assumed the drivers were taking a nap break in their trucks. All so innocent looking," she said.

"Then the raid happened and shut the amateur operation down," added Kyle.

I jumped in with a question. "What was the motivation for TBI to raid the place when it did?"

"An anonymous tip, of course," said Kyle, glancing at Ginny Faye.

With a sheepish grin, Ginny Faye explained, "I called Kyle, because we have been friends for years, for advice on what to do. He had heard rumors from other patrolmen and seen the bill boards so he believed me. He told me to keep quiet for my own protection and he would handle it, so I told him everything I knew about Josie, who was running the girls, and Mack's business flunky, who co-owned the gas station with him. Mack and his business partner were both indicted after the raid and paid a hefty fine, but the serious charges were dismissed. Josie was not present during the raid and not charged with anything. The phone number was disconnected and the trailers boarded up. A new sign was posted on the old gas station that read, "This is NOT a rest area. No trespassing." The truckers got the message and the whole thing should have been over. Y'all think it ended with the raid, but that was just the beginning of Mack's descent into crime," said Ginny Faye.

Kyle leaned in closer to Ginny Faye and asked, "So what happened after that?"

"Now this is the important part that y'all don't know so listen carefully. Long before the raid by TBI, the Memphis mafia got a whiff of Mack's and Josie's new prostitution business. They drove up from Memphis intending to scare them into closing shop. Instead of shutting them down the mob brokered a deal with Josie to coerce Mack into selling land to them, no questions asked. I could not figure out why they wanted land so far from Memphis, but they wanted it bad enough to pay ten times what the land was worth. Josie convinced Mack to sell them the five acre property where the oil business had once stood. Then Mack and Josie conspired to set up a fraud scheme to get rid of the oil company stockholders. The mafia wanted the land deal more than they wanted to eliminate the amateur prostitution location."

"And Josie got to keep her position as madam of the corrupted trailers," I said.

"Yes, our slippery bookkeeper managed to negotiate a cash deal with the mafia for the land. By this time, Josie was running the show. Mack gave her enough rope to hang him by going along with the fraud scheme and using the mafia money to build his first truck-stop. He lost touch with reality, but was getting rich."

I remembered my first interview with Ginny Faye when she revealed that Mack had built their first truck stop with cash from a dubious source.

"Please continue," I said.

"Okay," said Ginny Faye with a long exhale. "I'm trying to keep the facts in order so you will understand. Do you recall being told that a fire destroyed the first truck stop three years after it was built?"

I nodded my head while Kyle just waited for her to continue.

"Josie solicited the mafia to loan Mack money for the second truck stop. She had developed some kind of sick connection to them. The mob saw a perfect opportunity to launder a boatload of cash through Mack and they embraced Josie's twisted idea to make them more money. She needed the mob's power and connections to continue as a madam. The motel idea was hers, with girls out of Memphis provided by guess who? Mack altered the interior space and bribed the inspectors after the county planning commission signed off on the project."

Kyle's tone of voice was shocked and angry. "Mack learned nothing from the raid on the trailers. What a moron. His crime spree should have ended then if he had any sense."

"Mack's brains are made of money. His heart and feet are set in clay. Can't expect much from that combination," said Ginny Faye, who had more to tell.

"The mafia collects a low interest loan payment each month in cash, plus 75% of the gross profits from the motel. Josie keeps two sets of immaculate books. Mack still makes a boat load of illegal cash from his 25%. Josie earmarked Mack and his money for herself, long before our divorce. With the evidence she has on him, Mack would most likely go to prison the next time he is caught. So as long as they are lovers and partners in crime, he feels safe. Mack and Josie believed I was ignorant of everything. They never suspected me when the raid on the trailers happened."

I chimed in. "Josie has as much to lose as Mack if he goes to prison. She must have been stressed when the Judge gave you half the value of the truck stop. Losing control of that money had to hurt. She's got to blame somebody for her miserable failures."

Ginny Faye nodded in agreement to my summation. "That's the caveat in their relationship; they're double-crossing each other. Mack never intended to marry her. That's why he dragged our divorce to the edge of his grave for six years. If he goes to prison, he loses the other half of the truck stop. Josie believes she is the great manipulator of his life because she has a paper trail of his deals."

Her next statement was amazing to me and Kyle. "They have no clue that I possess a detailed copy of the bastardized blueprints for the truck stop, plus a full set of keys to the offices. I raked through her files more than once. How else could I know so much? So how is that for having a couple of aces up my sleeve?"

"Or at least one Ace," I said, with a smile from me.

Chapter 15

Ginny Faye had dropped a bomb. The fallout vibrated throughout the nearly empty room. I got excited thinking about all that evidence sitting in Josie's office. We all agreed that a subpoena for a search warrant would be necessary to bring Mack and Josie from the dark side into the light of justice. I thanked Kyle and Ginny Faye for the awesome interview, hoping there was a spark between them. They shared Jackson as their hometown and each had a daughter the same age. On top of that, Kyle was protective of her with animosity toward Mack. Being single and born in the same decade made them a good match, like my parents. I grudgingly left the peaceful scene with them smiling at each other.

* * *

My drive that afternoon from Jackson to Turtle Creek was tail-gated by bad weather. A battle between two fronts was imminent. If tornadoes were involved, there would be a warring that would destroy any resistance on the ground. The forecast for heavy storms, moving from west of the Mississippi River into middle Tennessee was a sure bet, considering the dew point and temperature range. I wanted to go straight home but knew better than to arrive half-empty. Dad expected his borrowed cars to come back with a full tank.

The next exit with petrol turned out to be Mack Mill's truck stop. I had seen the monstrosity from the road several times but never up-close. Morbid curiosity won out over caution. I followed the exit ramp to a truckers paradise. On this Sunday afternoon, the crowded interstate had thinned out. Big rigs were sparse in the parking lot with a few cars scattered in front of the restaurant. I chose a pump far away from the front door, put on a billed cap and contemplated the lay-out while trying to look casual. Sweat was beading under my armpits and the generic cap.

The main building was a typical design for a massive truck stop: square, well-lit and grotesque. There was no sign of a motel. The smell of diesel fuel cut through the humid air, assailing my nostrils. The sounds of idling engines and air brakes droned and hissed around me. The fumes were awful and might be what induced my temporary insanity to sleuth around.

A clerk accepted cash for the gas at his booth without making eye contact and I thought he might have been sleeping. Without exchanging a word, I accepted my change. Having a dealer tag with scribbled writing would deter anyone tracking my car. I pretended to walk toward my nondescript Honda, but at the last moment made a sharp right turn and walked around the rear corner of the large building. My covert move was a huge disappointment. Nothing much was there. What was I expecting? A motel with a red light over the door?

The back of the building showed four heavy metal doors facing a cow pasture. The blacktop, for trucks to make deliveries, extended about half the size of a football field from the back of the building to the pasture fence. Several halogen lights stood tall and bright. The only things on the parking pad were various piles of stacked wooden pallets and commercial trash bins.

The four doors were spaced about twenty feet apart, each labeled with a different sign. "Danger! High Voltage Electrical Equipment" was on door one, bordered by red, yellow and black stripes. Door two was marked "Private, Staff," with a keypad to enter a code. Door three was marked "Restaurant Delivery," with a large button to buzz and door four was marked "Storage and Trash," also with a keypad. The only door with no access from outside was the voltage door and who in their right mind would touch it?

Was the warning a ruse? Could the motel be on the other side of that door being used only for an exit? My imagination was running amok. I took pictures of each door with my cell phone then scurried back to my car, like a coon on the prowl.

The time used to snoop around back had only taken a couple of minutes, but my confidence had been raised to the idiot level on the bravery scale. Those diesel fumes were really doing a job. Instead of leaving, I moved the car from the gas pumps to the front of the building, got out again and strolled inside for a look around, like any other customer would.

"May I help you Sir?" asked a pimple-faced, skinny teenager with shiny braces.

"Just need the men's room."

"Straight ahead, turn left, second door on the right," he said.

I forged ahead, turned left and applied the brakes.

Suddenly my bravery scale dropped to busted. Mack Mills was standing in front of me about twenty feet away. He was talking to a woman, actually whispering in her ear and she was eating it up. I immediately did a 180 degree turn in the opposite direction, only to cross paths in front of a burly trucker on his way to the head. We side-stepped together, him left, me right, throwing the over-weight man off balance.

"Wanna dance?" the guy growled.

He proceeded to knock over a display of Slim Jims, skidding on the round sticks, then colliding into a rack of magnets made to look like baby license plates. I was half way to the front exit before the trucker hit the floor. The only thing I showed was my ass booking through the double doors.

My heart was thumping loud enough to be heard without a stethoscope when I got in my car, zoomed out of the parking lot and onto the interstate. Whew! What a rush of adrenaline and information in one afternoon. I wondered if the woman getting her ear tickled was Josie Cagle.

My smiling turned into giggles. Couldn't hold it back. All that pent up tension exploded out of me in full blown guffaws with tears rolling down my face. I never had more fun in my life and couldn't stop laughing for a full minute.

* * *

A thick veil of pink haze blocked the setting sun behind me as I drove on to Turtle Creek. The days were shorter in August but not any cooler. The air felt heavy and hard to breathe. A summer storm would come later tonight after the build-up of humidity could not be contained any longer. I was relieved to arrive home before dark.

Dry lightning started at dusk, turning the sky from pink to a sickening yellow. Next came rumbles of thunder, like a man's stomach before intestinal flu, except this was more ominous. Tornado warnings were out all over the state west of the Tennessee River and the storms continued to march eastward.

We finished dinner, but barely. While we were clearing the dishes off the table the sirens over the firehouse started screaming. Like London during the blitz, we had heard them before. The sound demanded a visit to our storm cellar via a trap door in the middle of the house. We scuttled down the stairs and settled in with full stomachs.

This safe place offered a good opportunity to talk about serious matters. I owed an explanation to Mom and Dad. Before trusting them with all the facts, I swore them to secrecy. I dumped on them, like the clouds dumping rain outside. My parents are great listeners.

The all-clear siren went off about an hour later. I had filled the cellar with the whole truth uncovered to-date. The summer storm was over for tonight but my fire-storm was just winding up.

Chapter 16

Raiding Josie's office at the truck stop was the least of my problems after I got back to Turtle Creek. Monday morning found Loretta sick in bed with the flu and not likely to make an appearance in the office for several days. The paper had to be printed every week, come hell or high water and James, her husband, needed help. It was going to be a long week at the Post Gazette. I threw myself into the task and learned more about being an editor in four days than I dreamed was possible.

About the time I thought I'd lose my mind, Loretta came back on Friday, thank God. The paper was distributed in time for James to get sick the next day. For half of the next week, I did his job as well as my own. Labor Day weekend was coming up fast which meant a short week with a pared down paper to get out in one less day. Everyone was on edge.

Kyle called out of the blue to ask how things were going. Instead of saying "fine" and letting him talk, I confessed my stupidity.

"I made a mistake and stopped at Mack's truck stop two weeks ago. I needed to get that off my chest. I'm sure nobody saw me."

"I don't care about your visit to the truck stop. Listen Ace," and he proceeded to hurl a grenade into our conversation.

"What if the shooter was not a man? And what if "she" owned a motorcycle, knew how to shoot and shopped in the boy's department? Josie had reason to hate Judge Lester after he awarded all that money to Ginny Faye. That right there was motive and I found an old record of assault," he said.

I was dumbfounded and waited for Kyle to speak.

His clairvoyant disclosure continued, "I figure she and half the county own a shot gun, but a 20 gauge is the perfect size for a woman to handle, especially if it's sawed off. You, Ace, are not the only one hanging out at the truck stop. I also ran the license plate of a Harley parked in the employee lot and guess who it belongs to? None other than Josie Cagle. And that's not all. Her trade mark fashion color is black, including the motorcycle and helmet hanging on the handlebar. I would bet on the nag if she was running in a horse race."

Excited, I responded, "You have no idea how much I want to agree with you. A missing link of information has been evading me for weeks and now I know what it was. Those damn deerskin gloves. No guy would be wearing them unless he was from England. I should have shown you the photo a long time ago."

"Now, said Kyle, what are we going to do about it? That locked office is not going to open itself. TBI could get another tip from me and raid the truck stop, but the contents of those files could disappear faster than dew in the desert if they got wind of it."

"Maybe a diversion could be created for me to sneak in and empty the drawers. Mack still does not know who I am," I said.

"Never would work and I don't want you shot. You don't know anything about sneaking around, much less how to defend yourself. I have another idea. A buddy from my former unit has special skills. With keys and blueprints to the office, he could take photos of the original documents. Nobody knows him and the contents of the room would look undisturbed. No harm, no foul. Then you can show up with the evidence for the DA and let him enforce the law with a search warrant. Do not tell anybody what I just told you until I have a chance to contact my friend. Then we can call Ginny Faye for the keys and blueprints. Let me be the middle man and plan the mission. That way, Josie and Mack will never see us coming until it's too late."

"Just exactly what did you do in the Army?" I asked.

"Army Rangers. The rest is classified."

"Do you really think Ginny Faye is in danger?"

"Yes. I think Josie is mean enough to turn that gun on anybody who gets in her way. Ginny Faye told me why she moved to Jackson. Josie threatened her. The rental house in Turtle Creek had developed a warped front door that didn't lock. She didn't feel safe. Her cheap-ass landlord refused to replace the door. She wisely decided to move out of town until the divorce was over. Ginny Faye loves living in Jackson. She has new friends, church support and she is miles away from Mack, who may be the lesser threat."

"Sounds like you two bonded after I left," I said.

"Don't go there," said Kyle. He hung up.

As usual, the Transformer had the last word.

Chapter 17

With all the planned activities, Labor Day is not a day of rest for every one in Turtle Creek. The parade committee commandeers every convertible in town and starts decorating on Friday for the Monday parade. A beauty queen is crowned Miss Labor Day on Saturday. Traffic lights are reset to blink red for an hour, snarling vehicles in all directions until the parade ends. Both of the county high school bands perform, one leading and the other bringing up the rear. The mayor waves to the spectators from a fancy car somewhere in the middle. Local clubs and organizations fill in the gaps, from the Masons to the Cub Scouts. Kids and adults enjoy the last free weekend of summer while dreading the new school year beginning on Tuesday. Lots of family reunions are planned over the course of the long weekend and every church sponsors a dinner on the grounds after Sunday services.

I invited Sandra as my guest. She showed up with two casseroles in tow, impressing the heck out of my mother. Folding tables were covered with chicken and dressing, fried okra, beef-steak sliced tomatoes, creamed corn and deviled eggs just to name my favorites. Other tables groaned with banana pudding, fresh strawberry pie, coconut and chocolate cakes, brownies and cookies. Church ladies know how to cook.

After eating way too much, we sat in her car and talked about our families. I asked Sandra how on earth her mother, Ginny Faye, found the strength to endure the six year divorce.

"Mom is simply my hero," said Sandra. "Not once did she curse Mack or wish him dead. I can't say the same for me. Instead, she prayed for him and relied on her incredible faith to bring her through. But don't get the wrong idea when it comes to Josie. Mom regrets the day they gave her a job as their bookkeeper. A person like Josie, who is eaten up with jealously, is rotten to the core. I can't fathom what Mack sees in her."

Prostitution and profits or prison and poverty, I thought. The four P's of a pitiful relationship not about to blow over any time soon. I couldn't tell Sandra the truth, how Kyle had figured Josie out, until we had proof.

"Keep your distance and avoid any confrontation with Josie," I warned.

* * *

I didn't hear from Kyle for two weeks. He finally called to set up a rendezvous to go over a plan that was not appropriate for discussion on the phone. Kyle's directions led me west of Turtle Creek on I-40 to a non-populated exit, bearing right on a two lane road. The deserted farm, 1.2

miles on my left was my destination, with instructions to pull behind the house for obvious reasons. I parked where I was told, lowered the window, cut the engine and fidgeted on alert mode. The place was overgrown, littered with broken equipment and gaping holes in the barn's roof. The scene was downright eerie. The quiet was overwhelming. No barking dog, no road noise, no nothing. There are hundreds of deserted farms like this one in the South.

Suddenly two spooked doves took off in front of me. I could hear the flap of their wings from fifty yards away. Two men walked out of the barn at the same time. I swallowed hard and adjusted my glasses as I recognized Kyle. Only then did I get out of the car and walk toward the barn. We walked inside the roofless structure where they had hidden their car. The stranger with Kyle looked me over while I was checking him out too.

"This is Major John Masters, retired army officer and trusted friend. Meet A. C. King, the best investigative reporter I have met in a long time," said Kyle.

I shook hands with both men, holding eye contact with Masters.

"Kyle told me everything he knows about you and this mission, but I have a few questions before we get started. Like why are you pursuing this? Have you been affected directly and what is your motive?" asked John.

The questions were legitimate and deserved to be answered.

"Like you sir, I have a duty to protect innocent people and right a wrong if I can. Exposing the truth is only part of my job as a reporter. The other part is being able to live with myself if I don't follow through. Call me Ace and tell me your plan."

The plan was simple, as plans should be. John would furtively enter the truck stop, having memorized the floor plan and possessing keys to the locked vaults of information. After photographing the original documents on micro film, he would leave them arranged in their proper order. The operation would be done late at night, concise, and finished quickly because he had done this type of mission many times. Any weapons would be noted but untouched. He would turn the damning proof over to me and Kyle and we would go directly to the DA.

After the mission, John would disappear, like the ghost he had always been. My orders were to keep my mouth shut until the evidence was delivered to me. I had no intention of saying anything to anyone. We parted as obscurely as we had arrived. The only witnesses to our meeting were two doves.

PART II

Southern Hostility

Chapter 18
Lucius—The Memphis Godfather

Perched on the mighty Mississippi River, Memphis is politically correct with a black mayor, black police chief and mostly all black police force. According to the latest census, the metropolitan population is 65% black, controlling almost everything in Memphis, including the vice crimes in the city. The main syndicate is a mob, who not only corrupt Memphis and Shelby County, but infest counties east to the Tennessee River. They manage to run law enforcement ragged in Memphis and beyond.

The head of this syndicate is Lucius Hogg, the holy-terror version of a Godfather, better known as Big Pig, with a reputation of effectively eliminating anyone who sticks their nose into his territory. His loyal lieutenants answer directly to Lucius, come when he calls and do whatever he demands. Today, they were meeting at a barbeque joint with some of the best pulled pork in the world. Carrying plenty of fire power tucked in all kinds of places on their bodies was the norm.

After their food orders were in, Chickie Smith, one of his lieutenants mouthed off. "Listen up bros. We need to make more money turning tricks. Y'all got any new ideas on how to increase revenue, cause we ain't making enough money in this particular endeavor? Ain't that right, Boss?"

The other endeavors included money laundering, carjacking, home invasions, distribution of drugs, extortion and gambling.

Lucius glared at Chickie for speaking out of turn. He stabbed his fork on the table to get their attention and said, "What we need to do is control more locations by training new girls in the fine art of madam-hood. There's no end to the hos willing to work, but they need leadership from madams who know their stuff."

"Yeah," said Chickie, "I only know one piece of work that fits that description. You saying we need to hire more lily-white butts like hers to run our business?"

"I'm saying, that if you keep on acting scared of that white woman I may demote you right back to selling on a corner. Then you can move back in yo momma's house," said Lucius. "You hear me?"

Chickie never knew how to respond to his boss so he nodded, smacking his lips shut. Lucius knew his crew were in awe of Josie Cage. Hell, who wouldn't be? She was his golden goose, making him lots of money managing a successful whore house. When the food arrived on big trays accompanied by pitchers of beer and lots of sticky sauce, they dove in and ate, like pigs at a trough.

Lucius was thirty four, a decade older than his top men and a confirmed bachelor. When they kowtowed to him out of fear and reverence, he sometimes felt like their father. Before turning twenty, he had pimped his own sisters right under their grandmother's nose, then added drug dealing in his pathetic ghetto neighborhood. He knew he could have it all in Memphis by the time he turned twenty-five. Tired of paint ball games and violent videos, he signed up for shooting lessons at a local gun range. With no police record ten years ago, he legally bought as many different guns as he wanted at out-of-state gun shows. His hoard of over two hundred pieces would be the envy of any collector. Learning how to correctly use and clean every one of them became his passion.

A second, secret passion, a real weak spot he was ashamed of because he was black, took him by surprise.

His gun instructor, Kelly, at the Hot Shot Range, taught him everything about marksmanship. She had no clue that his heart had been turned into mush. The problem was her being white. Throughout his life, Lucius grew up in a black world, interacting little with Caucasians. He never dreamed of being touched by a white woman as part of the instruction process at the rifle and gun range.

Kelly left him breathless when she whispered instructions, while correcting his stance or hold on the weapon. Her touch was light as a feather, as if he were receiving a blessing from above. Lucius was aware it was not sexual, but felt touched inside his psyche, causing him to question his inborn prejudices.

With hair the color of corn silks and hands the same color on both sides, Kelly haunted him at night. Holding her dainty sunglasses on a turned up petite nose was unlike the flared nostrils of his kind. Wearing protective head gear afforded no huge hoop earrings or multiple piercings. Only clear polish adorned her short, clean nails and she smelled like soap instead of cheap perfume. The soft tone of her voice, speaking in a regal southern accent was comforting and soothing. She was the most natural human being he had ever met. Fragile, like a small kitten or a puppy for Lucius to protect. Nothing like the black women he knew. Lucius was in love, but he kept it to himself, because he did not understand the feelings and never would..

His henchmen used regular smart phones with their girlfriends and mammas on speed dial, but business between the mob was done on throw away phones. They were regularly destroyed to hide the evidence they contained. Lucius had expanding ideas for his syndicate rolling around in his head like ball bearings in a lazy Susan. One of his ideas was to find a place far removed from

Memphis and the prying eyes of law enforcement to dispose of incriminating evidence.

Getting richer every day, Lucius was "high on the hog", as they say in the South. Greed and pride had already pushed his ambitions east of Memphis, before he learned about his newest competition, a prostitution venture that had sprung up near the Tennessee River.

Chapter 19
Lucius and Josie

Not only was Lucius fascinated, but he was also furious when he first heard about two billboard signs on Interstate 40 advertising services for truckers. Who had the balls to do something that brazen and get away with it? Competition in the territory claimed by him had to be dealt with swiftly.

When he called the number on the sign, hearing the message, a white woman with a red-neck accent promising to call back, he left a number which was returned by Josie Cagle. Lucius made it clear they needed to meet privately and talk business. After agreeing on a date and time, Josie directed him to the Blue Bird Boat Dock exit, on the west side of the Tennessee River. A dirt packed turn-around about a quarter mile from the dock was the meeting spot. They circled their vehicles so they could talk from each drivers window, letting their engines idle and sizing each other up.

Some gangs adopt code names to distinguish themselves, but Lucius had personal cards printed with a logo from a 60's T V show, "Have Gun Will Travel". The card was black with white lettering and featured a golden bullet in one corner. No name or contact information was included, but the corny card spoke for itself. Lucius twirled the card between his fingers before extending his arm far enough for her to take it.

"Cute," she said, " and your point is?"

"Do you have a clue who I am?"

"Duh, your card has no name on it."

"I'm Lucius Hogg, aka "Big Pig" in Memphis, and your worst nightmare, unless you have something I want. Do you understand anything so far or should I spell it out, you dumb broad."

The sawed off shotgun was in her window before Lucius got dumb broad out of his mouth. He froze. She didn't blink. The gun was close enough to blow his head off, but her warning came first.

"Now, you were saying, 'big pig', that understanding was important, so understand this. You tell me who you are and what you're after or else. Are we clear?"

Lucius held up both hands wearing flashy diamonds that matched the one in his left earlobe, then rested them on his steering wheel. He wondered what he was thinking when he left Memphis without a body guard. He would never understand white women. Did they all carry guns? Lucius had a big shoulder gun strapped on but not a lap dog like hers, so he had no choice but to chill and talk with the gun leveled at his throat.

No problem, just negotiations like two rival gang leaders.

Suddenly a strange thing happened. He started to have respect for this gun-toting mama with attitude, recognizing raw talent when he saw it. Here was an opportunity to help him move a problem outside of Memphis and he decided to try and make a deal.

"I'm looking to buy some property near the Tennessee River for cash. I might look the other way concerning your business if you can direct me to a seller," said Lucius.

"I thought we were coming to an understanding about my right to operate my whore house without your interference," Josie said. "What are you even talking about?"

"Do you have access to a vacant piece of property or not?" he pressed.

Agitated, Josie sneered and asked, "What the hell do you plan to do with property this far from Memphis? Build the east wing of Elvis's mansion and open your own whore house?"

"Now calm down lady. No building is going on the property. I just need the necessary seclusion for private business meetings and a passable dirt road for vehicles. That's all," explained Lucius.

"Really?" she said, not convinced yet.

Although she eyed him suspiciously, he surmised she was considering the idea. While waiting for a response, he kept his hands in view, eyes front, calmly studying the diamond rings.

"How much money are you talking about and how much land do you need? For the right price, I might have exactly what you want, plus a hands-off policy concerning my trailers and girls. Who, by the way, are out of Nashville. They are no threat to your West Tennessee operation."

Holy mother, this is one cocky white woman, thought Lucius. He responded carefully.

"Depends on the location, but three to five acres should be plenty and I can be generous with my cash if I'm getting what I want," said Lucius.

"Yeah, well I'm thinking of some river-front property, but it won't be cheap. You would have to sign a contract with a rider agreement to leave my business alone. We both get a copy for obvious reasons. You disappear. That's what I want," said Josie.

"Before I sign anything, I need to see the land. It has to be very private, no close neighbors, clear of liens or Indian burial grounds. Pausing for a second, Lucius asked, "Do I have to worry about the owner or do you control him too?"

"I'm his bookkeeper, lover and madam. I know for a fact that he will gladly take your money. Be ready to pay cash when I confirm the price. Call me in one week for the trade. Your money for a clean deed. Goodbye Mr. Hogg."

Josie had not lowered the gun or eased up on the trigger. Lucius had not relaxed a curly hair on his head, but knew they had struck a deal. He got his way and would live to tell about it. She had simply dismissed him, "The Memphis Godfather", watching him drive away. He had been burned, like a biscuit with a black bottom.

If ever Lucius saw a freak of nature, Josie Cagle fit the bill. A white Godmother. He chuckled at the irony and looked forward to further contact with the ballsy broad.

Chapter 20
Josie—The Other Woman

Resetting the safety, she lowered the gun back to her lap and watched Lucius drive away. No doubt he was a dangerous and powerful man, as she studied the encrypted card he had handed over, reminding her of Graceland's owner.

Smiling, Josie thought of Elvis Presley's black card with a white lightning bolt and letters, TCOB, standing for, "Taking Care Of Business". He had his own mob from 1957-1977, a bunch of want-to-be hoods, who dressed all in black to protect the "King" from evil forces, like the real mafia in Las Vegas. What a joke. She wondered how many women they commandeered to protect Elvis.

Josie slammed her foot down hard on the accelerator, spinning wheels and throwing dirt as she headed for the Interstate. Flipping her satellite radio to country music and cranking the volume up, she barreled down the road. Driving fast was when she did her best scheming. She was doing more than considering Lucius' offer. Her trap-door mind was fixated on an appalling piece of land owned by Mack Mills. The site had been a depository for fuel oil, useless now since the soil was no doubt polluted from leaky underground tanks. She couldn't wait to tell Mack, that he was about to be richer. The faster she drove the more new ideas poured into her conniving brain.

Josie Cagle was a piece of work with a head messed up since childhood. School bullies had teased and called her names like Trashy and Dirtbag, because her father was the janitor at school. Her mother, extremely obese, died from an exhausted heart before turning forty, providing another brunt of teasing from her classmates. Josie was ashamed of both parents, becoming a bully herself, a logical transition for a girl with low self-esteem and no hope of being accepted by her peers. Manipulation of other people's lies and secrets had turned her into a friendless person.

She liked being a bookkeeper and was good at the task, sequestered alone in an office with only occasional contact with other people. Being in control of the records gave her a semblance of the power that had been stripped away years ago.

When the flirtatious handsome boss, Mack Mills, began making advances, she decided to maintain control of the relationship. He was married and she did not want to lose her job over a fling, so she resisted his advances. Josie pretended to befriend his wife as she watched how he treated her, while waiting for a chance to trap Mack into her web. Two years later she discovered tax evasion and money laundering in his books. Mack had hidden investments all over the place, including the cash purchase of two trailers being used for prostitution. That is when she made her move. After bedding him far better than he imagined, she told him what she wanted; a promotion with a 25% salary increase, including management of the prostitution location. She reasoned that supervising a whore house by a woman made more sense. Realizing her potential, he readily agreed to the proposal.

Mack also went along with the deal Josie contracted with the mob and he was impressed with the sizable amount of cash she brokered for the worthless land. Together, they produced a phony land deed for Lucius, and used the all cash payment to build a truck stop. The books were in the black from year one. Josie took over the prostitution business at the trailers with no more interference from the Memphis mob. She sequestered the damning paperwork in her locked office files, putting Mack Mills under her control.

Josie had collected lovers, like empty beer cans over the years. She preferred affairs with married men, because they were vulnerable to blackmail and willing to pay when she threatened to tell their wives. In reality, she hated men, but loved moving them around like pawns on a game board.

Her plan to wreck Mack's life slowly changed when she recognized he was like her; a user, a taker and a hater of most people. Plus, he was getting richer every year and threw his new money around like a possessed man while she was not getting any younger. Her face and figure were sagging along with her bank account, so she put Mack in her sights as the ultimate trophy, threw a net over his finances and hunkered down, waiting for his divorce to be final.

Chapter 21
Ginny Faye Mills

When a wife discovers her husband is having an affair, she does one of two things. She falls apart or exacts revenge. Denial usually occurs before the rage sets in, which is exactly what happened to Ginny Faye when she heard about the betrayal. Her world, as she knew it, collapsed. The material things, holding up her marriage, were just props in a play about a tragic relationship. Mack pulled the blinds shut on her sanity, like Satan did to Eve. She couldn't reason or think rationally because she had never been allowed to before. All she could do was pray for wisdom and peace, on her knees with lots of tears. Belief in God's help was a constant, but what she needed was relief from the pain.

The one person Ginny Faye trusted was her daughter, Sandra, who told her mother about Mack's affair. Josie deliberately leaked the information to get the ball rolling. Ginny Faye did not want to believe the awful news as her heart was being ripped apart, but she knew her daughter was telling the truth. To make matters worse, Mack didn't lie when she confronted him.

The next phase, bargaining with Mack, did not work, so she fled her country home and rented a house in Turtle Creek. Mack was angry, but believed she would fold, come home and accept his decision to have a paramour and a wife. Ginny Faye's life was like a yo-yo until she made the decision to put some distance between herself and Mack's affair with Josie. Leaving Fairfax county was the answer. Common sense returned after the move to Jackson and she felt safe enough to file divorce papers with a sympathetic lawyer, Richard Pruitt, representing her. That's when the long haul in court began.

Ginny Faye's first marriage to a Mr. French, occurred when she was too young to have common sense. The one good thing to come out of that marriage was her daughter, Sandra. The lazy, immature husband was an abuser of the bruising variety. Not knowing that she had rights, she might have allowed the beatings to continue until he killed her, except for her daddy. He intervened with a two-by-four, driving the no-account, sloth of a husband out the door. And since her father was a Baptist preacher, he told the man to go straight to hell. Mr. French never came back. Divorce papers arrived a year later, giving her full custody of her daughter, but no child support from the dead-beat dad. He had moved out of state with another unsuspecting woman.

Cooking fine Southern food was Ginny Faye's talented gift. Within five years, after her marriage ended, she had established herself as head chef of an up-scale restaurant in Nashville. She was a single parent trying to make ends meet when Mack Mills walked into her restaurant to behold an angel wearing an apron.

Chapter 22
Mack Mills

Taken by surprise, Mack saw past an apron covering a voluptuously gorgeous figure and past a hair net containing long, golden curls. Gazing into her violet eyes, the color of Elizabeth Taylor's, Mack was lost. She had a voice that dripped of honey and warm butter. All he thought about was getting her in bed, but her Christian morals held him at bay. When he could stand it no longer, they were married. Because of her Baptist upbringing, he never believed she would divorce him for any reason. Ginny Faye's beauty and charm made him look good. Everyone took to her except Mack's jealous mother, whose vote didn't count anyway.

Always intense, Mack had a deep furrow between his eyes that warned people, like a blinking red light. Since he never looked relaxed, he was not considered a handsome man, appearing rather ordinary with average height and weight, limp brown hair and mean eyes. A small mustache hid a thin upper lip over straight teeth. The money clip in his pocket, holding a big wad of greenbacks, did the talking for him.

His inflated ego included a sense of royal entitlement, with a King Midas persona. Money was the only friend he wanted. Puffing out his chest was an exercise for Mack Mills. He collected a lot of business acquaintances, but few friends. For the drawn out divorce, Mack hired Phyllis Faulkner, who came highly recommended. She was a take-no-prisoners advocate for rich men who didn't love their wives enough to share their wealth after a divorce. Mack assumed his lawyer knew he was protecting more than his money. He met his lawyer's requests to involve Josie, his partner in crime, with stubborn indignation because he feared she would expose his secrets if ever called as a witness. Mack had chosen well with Phyllis as his lawyer because her hands were buried deep in his pockets. She would ride it out for the long haul just like Ginny Faye. A mean spirited man preferred giving money to anyone before his wife.

Women had always been his biggest problem throughout life starting with his hovering mother. She smothered him and micro-managed his entire childhood until he broke away from her control. Never having sisters or aunts gave him no insight on how to treat other women with respect and dignity.

Acting on impulse when he was younger, he chose to have an affair with his neighbor's wife, regretting it immediately. The woman thought

Mack was in love with her after one roll under the covers. She told her husband, Tom Warren, that she was in love with Mack. Furious, Tom threw her out, sending her back to Mack with divorce papers, who freaked out when she wanted to get married and have a baby. Mack could not get rid of her until his mother kicked in with money to make her go away. When Tom would not take her back, she finally gave up and moved on. The bad feelings between the men never went away.

Mack vowed that he would never get married. Then he met the beautiful Ginny Faye French and fell in love. He was damn lucky that Tom didn't shoot him.

Chapter 23
Josie and Mack

Josie went straight to Mack with the offer from Lucius. They put their heads together hatching a plan and decided to fake a bankruptcy of the fuel oil business, scamming the stockholders. The rest was easy. Josie composed a convincing letter informing the stockholders of the failed attempt to revive the old business and the pressing need to get rid of the albatross by filing for bankruptcy. The bald face fabrication of the letter stated, "that to remove the underground tanks and risk polluting the surrounding soil and water table, was a violation of EPA regulations".

The lying letter was pure drivel to convince the stockholders that the land was worthless. After including an apology for their loss and imploring their understanding, Mack blamed his father, Frank, for having poor business sense which resulted in running the business to ground. Basically, he threw a dead man under the bus. The letter was pitiful, but it worked.

Josie and Mack had used the site many times to rendezvous. They would take off in the middle of the day, pretending a business run. Screwing around on the deserted plot of land was how Josie knew about the property. To seal the shady deal with Lucius, they had made up a phony deed for him to sign, who didn't know the difference between a manifesto and a French menu, much less an original deed. After the counterfeit document was signed and a massive amount of cash changed hands, Mack and Josie celebrated their success at a local dive bar over beers.

Chapter 24
Kyle Cunningham

Kyle and Mack were young boys when their fathers went into the fuel oil business together. They were not playmates then or friends later, since their families lived on opposite sides of the Tennessee River. The boys chose their careers after high school, with one serving himself and the other serving his country.

Kyle inherited the warrior gene, revering his twenty years in special forces, which resulted in a slew of metals that he never displayed. He had served as a legal gun runner for allied forces and carried out classified work for Black Hawk, a covert government contractor. Never a braggart, Kyle's bonus from Uncle Sam was coming home alive to his family. After his wife died of cancer, Kyle mourned for a long time. When the fog of grief began to lift, he perceived that the good women around his age were taken. Resigned to being alone, he gracefully accepted being a widower.

The pride of his life was his daughter, Kelly. He taught her to shoot and shoot well and could not be prouder if she had been a son. With his father suffering in the last stage of Alzheimer's, she was all the family he had left. After his last tour ended, he considered a job offer in Washington, D. C. with the FBI, but it was too far from his ailing father and daughter. His long time Army friend, John Masters, now a private investigator in Memphis, suggested Kyle apply with the State Police who snapped him up like a prize. At Kyle's request, they stationed him between Memphis and Jackson. Everyone was a winner when he took the job. He was happy to collect two pay checks a month; one from Uncle Sam and one from the State of Tennessee.

With great pleasure, he watched as Kelly matured, completing one goal after another. Observing her prepare for the Winter Olympics Biathlon event, combining cross-country skiing and target rifle shooting, delighted him. While earning a degree in criminal law from Memphis State, she also worked part-time at a local gun range, teaching marksmanship. Kyle was one proud father who would thwart any obstacle that got in his daughter's way.

His meeting with Ace enlightened him that Ginny Faye was divorced from Mack. Until the young reporter had interviewed him, Kyle did not know she resided in Jackson. Once, during her marriage to Mack, she had called him for advice, when the trailers of ill repute needed to be raided and shut down. She was trying to protect Mack from Josie's wacky need to run a whore house.

This was long before she found out about their affair.

Kyle's wife and Ginny Faye were friends in high school and saw each other at their class reunion every five years until Kyle's wife died. While Ginny Faye was married to her abusive husband, she confided in her girlfriend about the beatings from him. Kyle's wife persuaded Kyle to inform Ginny Faye's father, a stern Baptist preacher, to straighten him out. Kyle had hoped her life would get better after she divorced husband number one, but then Mack came along. Now she was single again and Kyle had taken notice. He knew the time had come to make his move on a woman he both admired and respected, hoping the feeling was mutual.

Chapter 25
The Lost Property

The tanker barges that had carried the oil from the northern pipeline south were equipped with big pumps to off load the fuel oil at various sub-stations located along the river. Frank's Fuel Oil was a sub-station at one point of delivery on the Tennessee river with underground holding tanks for the oil used to fill the trucks waiting above ground. The original location was washed out after heavy flooding destroyed the docks several years ago. The deliveries had ceased long before the flood occurred leaving little trace of anything on that stretch of the river.

A lot of undergrowth had consumed the area, including a narrow path from the river side to the former business site. Now the only access to the location was Tick Road, barely visible, paralleling the Buzzard Cave Boat Dock exit from Interstate 40. In the heyday of the business, the dirt road was packed down with gravel and functioned just fine for trucks. Now it was a not maintained and a muddy mess when wet. The road had crossed a bridge spanning the Fox River, providing Frank Mills a short-cut to his business by living so close to the bridge. His partner, Leon Cunningham, had to cross the Tennessee River to hook up with Tick Road.

The fuel oil business had been comprised of five acres fronting the Tennessee River owing to a land lease from the state of Tennessee. Neither Frank or Leon had ever owned the property or claimed to own it. The original lease's expiration date had ended around the time Frank died and then the property rolled over into the federal watershed conservation program that started in the 80's. The program continues to this day, protecting rivers and wildlife from exploitation and development for private use.

Mack wanted to believe that his father owned the riverfront property, even though a deed did not exist. He never imagined that an expired state lease was locked in his mothers safe. Unaware, he blatantly sold land in a water shed conservation district for cash, to the mafia.

State and federal agencies frown on these practices with steep penalties. Mack was on a slippery slope with a rope around his neck.

Chapter 26
Lucius and his mob

Lucius believed he was the proud owner of property on the Tennessee River. Busting to brag to somebody, he called for a meeting near the Naval Air Base north of Memphis. The location was a grass-choked former airstrip that allowed the public to watch jets come and go, day and night from the base. Tailgate parties were common with military families taking advantage of the free entertainment.

Three dark SUV s joined the crowd. Twelve men got out and stood with their boss pretending to watch the takeoffs and landings. Lucius showed them the newly minted deed, threatening a field trip next week for show and tell. He explained, over the sound of screaming jet engines, how the property would be used. His minions dreaded the two hour drive back and forth from Memphis to dispose of cell phones, guns and other incriminating evidence. They wisely hid their lack of enthusiasm, but Lucius knew how lazy they had become. They would do as he said, like it or not.

Lucius and his bodyguards had carefully inspected the acreage before exchanging cash for a deed. The buried tanks were an unexpected bonus. Josie promised that a special tool, to unlock the covers, would be included with the deed at closure. Confident that his men would have access to the tanks below ground, Lucius signed a bill of sale and relinquished the cash. Entombing the evidence, like burner phones and weapons, would be a lot easier with the tanks and safer from discovery than digging a hole in the ground.

The Mexican cartel, who had approached Lucius about distributing their drugs in West Tennessee, were pushing harder than ever. Certain that blacks and Mexicans could not work together, Lucius smelled a showdown coming soon. His current supply of drugs originated out of St. Louis or New Orleans and Lucius wanted to keep things the way they were. Barges moving north and south on the Mississippi river offered a much safer delivery than human mules crossing state lines between Texas and Memphis. No one searched barges loaded with grain. He had two river-boat captains in his back pocket. Who needed the Mexicans?

PART III

Southern Harmony

Chapter 27

When Cecil offered to be my guide on a river cruise, I immediately pictured myself on the TV show, "Survivor," aimlessly adrift on a big body of water with snakes crawling over the side of the boat. Shaking the image out of my head, I decided to give my friend an ear while having a little fun at his expense.

"So, you want to know where we're going or what?" Cecil asked.

"Let me guess. A canoe trip to the Promised Land, or are we going to Disney World?"

"Nobody likes a smart ass Ace. You just ruined my surprise."

"Okay, I'm a little bit sorry. Tell me more. Do I have to wear a parka?"

"We're not going duck hunting, you fool, and no bridges are involved."

Since Cecil was dead serious, I stopped goading him and tried to mimic his mood. He shared his new plan to motor down river where the Buzzard Cave boat docks were before the flood, then walk inland to find the lost property. Feeling nervous about dying, I asked about precautions.

"Look Ace, if you don't know how to handle a gun I won't give you one. Bring that fancy phone of yours with GPS. I'll bring a gun, just in case."

"Just in case of what? Moonshiners, the Mafia or starving to death?" I moaned.

"That's a good idea Ace, bringing a couple sacks of burgers from the Dairy Queen. We may be in the woods all day."

"Good Lord, I'm going to die young if I keep hanging out with you."

"How else you gonna find that place, Ace? Not by sitting in a dinky corner office. Get out, have some adventure, take some nature pictures and get a tan," declared Cecil.

Letting out a long sigh, I shook my hanging head from side to side and gave up. Cecil did have a good argument. During October, the trees were dropping their leaves, enhancing visibility. The reptiles were going underground because of cooler weather, but to be cautious, a new pair of high-top boots would be purchased tomorrow.

After deciding to go on Saturday, three days away, we hung up. The incredible weather forecast promised to deliver an Indian Summer weekend with a Canadian high pressure over the entire south.

Not taking any risks this time, I informed my parents of the new plan and asked them to have a helicopter on stand-by. They were not even mildly amused. I had been an Eagle Scout at one time, but had seldom used any of the skills after earning all those badges. Instead, I had turned into a spongy geek.

* * *

Cecil drove his pick-up, towing a fishing boat with a small motor. His truck must have been found at a war-zone sale. The body was repainted with a camouflage pattern and rolled on all-terrain, monster tires. Double pairs of spot lights were mounted on top of the cab. Bullet holes showed in the front grill which required baling wire to hold the thing together. We picked up our gourmet, carry-out lunches from the DQ and headed for Chiggerville State Park. My new boots and a hunting cap, purchased at Wal-Mart, completed my look. I wondered if Cecil would notice that I had managed to match his truck. Maybe no one would recognize me behind the heavily tinted, reflective sunglasses.

"Why are you scooted down in the seat?" asked Cecil.

"Just trying to get my sore hip comfortable," I lied.

"That thing still giving you trouble? Try sleeping with a pillow between your knees. Stay low and I'll drive slow."

* * *

Arriving at our destination, we found the park crowded with weekend warriors dressed like us.

Cecil backed the trailer down the ramp, then waited while I unhooked the boat before sliding the craft onto the water. After parking his excuse for a truck, retrieving water bottles and the bag of burgers, we were on our way. The river was warm and calm with a glassy surface; a perfect day to water ski. I was able to relax as we glided along while Cecil pointed out duck blinds, a pair of soaring eagles, a century old log cabin and other points of interest.

About a mile from our starting point at the state park, we saw some old pilings sticking out of the water, announcing our destination. Cecil steered the boat in that direction, cut the motor and drifted onto a gravel bar. The location was beautiful, ablaze with fall colors reflecting on the water which was gently lapping against the shore. We stepped out and pulled the boat farther into some tall weeds, hiding it from would-be thieves. Throwing an army green net over the outboard motor and hull was a successful disappearing trick. The boat and motor would take a little nap while we took a walk-about.

Wandering into the woods, we spotted a lone telephone pole and headed that way. Stepping out of the woods revealed an old dirt road, primitive, like a logging trail for oxen, narrow and muddy, but showing tire tracks.

"See, you of little faith. I told you so," bragged Cecil.

"Don't even think about preaching to me until we actually find the place. Which way do we go? Left or Right? I don't see any more poles. If we guess wrong, we could get in trouble again."

Being overly dramatic, Cecil raised both arms to heaven imploring, "What are you afraid of? There is nobody out here for miles around but us."

"I don't care. This place is spooky. You're the master woodsman so I expect you to guide us to the spot. Then let's clear out of here, before the Mafia shows up."

Cecil stared at me and I felt a twinge of shame for my lack of courage.

Finally he said "Follow me and learn. We'll walk ten minutes in one direction. If we don't find the place on the first try we can turn around and walk in the other direction. This shouldn't take long and I suspect it's close to the river, where the off loading docks used to be. There's no way we can go wrong if we stay on the road."

Using his big knife, Cecil marked our starting point on a cedar tree.

Within minutes we heard an echo of our walking sound. When Cecil abruptly stopped and listened, I nearly walked into his backside. He had one hand on his knife and the other was holding a rifle on his shoulder. He shushed me with a quick motion to his lips and I obeyed. Slowly he pivoted his big body and looked behind me.

"RUN!" he said, taking off like a Nike commercial.

Feet, don't fail me now! I picked up my new boots in double-time.

Charging forward, we didn't stop until we ran into and then up the side of a chain link fence. Looking back over my shoulder, I saw what Cecil had seen to set him off.

Feral hogs, and they wanted our lunch.

Both of us were hanging on to the top of a swaying section of chain-link fence with a hairy herd snorting at our heels. Convinced they were ready to eat us, I was filled with motivation and flew over the top of that fence like the Eagle Scout that I am. Cecil let out a blood curdling yell and morphed into a Ninja warrior, firing his rifle straight up as he came over the seven foot fence. Hogs cannot fly or climb fences so they backed off and we were safe, for now.

Looking around, we saw more of the fence on the ground than standing. It was an uh-oh moment as we realized it would only take a few minutes for the herd to figure out an end run. The good news was that we had found the lost property. Hallelujah!

Knowing the hogs were territorial animals with nasty tempers, Cecil fired off back-to-back shots and they scattered, barely hidden along the edge of the tree line. We stayed close to the fence in case we had to get off the ground again.

Cecil reloaded. We waited. Only one reappeared; the biggest, ugliest thing imaginable, with sharp tusks protruding from each side of a drooling mouth. Squealing and pawing, the alpha male beast was challenging us.

Aiming his rifle at the real estate in front of the hog's front hooves, Cecil fired, propelling a lot of dirt into the stupid animal's eyes. The reaction was a violent shaking of his hideous head while backing up into the brush with the sound of the herd retreating in the distance. Cecil promised they were gone for good.

I had been holding my breath and was still squeezing the fence with my fingers when I asked in a squeaky voice, "Did you mean to kill him and miss?"

"I don't miss and the hog was not game today. Live and let live for another day. Want to eat lunch now?"

God knows I have never been hungrier because of the adrenaline rush. Leaning against the metal fence, we gobbled down the cold food, followed by loud burps. Wadding our paper wrappers, Cecil stuffed them in the waterproof lining of his backpack. We chased the burgers with bottles of lukewarm water. Food never tasted so good.

By our estimate, the formerly enclosed area was less than an acre. After inspecting every inch of the property, we failed to turn up a gum wrapper, cigarette butt or beer can. The double gates lay on the ground where the front entrance used to be. Lots of saw-grass had filled in the open area, along with young trees, but the tops of the vented, underground tanks still protruded above ground. Evidence showed recent visitors from more than one vehicle's tire tracks. The four vent tops, indicating how many tanks were underground, had been man-handled, showing dirty smears in an attempt to open them. I took pictures of everything from all directions while Cecil worked in vain to pry open the vents with his hands. Each cover was round, shaped like a man-hole cover and appeared to be frozen shut. The openings would be about a foot across when the tops were fully up. A special key-like tool would be needed to unlock the covers. After capturing close-up photos of the strange locks on the covers, we had nothing else to see. Vacating the property, we retraced our steps the same way we had walked in.

Following the fresh tire tracks on the muddy road led us to Buzzard Cave Road which had an exit off the Interstate. Cecil marked the hike with fresh cuts on other cedar trees along the way.

"Now we can find the damn place without a boat," said Cecil.

"Yeah, I'm surprised that most of the telephone poles are gone. I only saw two standing. They looked puny compared to newer ones."

"Your powers of observation are improving Ace. I might make a woodsman outta you yet. Want me to teach you how to shoot?"

"Don't count on it. I think I broke my trigger finger while hanging onto that chain-link fence."

Cecil was chuckling to himself on our walk back to the waiting boat, ending our afternoon adventure.

The shadows had grown long and a cool breeze was scattering leaves on the water while our sputtering motor boat took us back to the launch point. I knew too much about this story to keep it to myself and pondered how to proceed next.

Chapter 28

The time had come to inform Chief Herring of my discoveries or at least part of them. I was sure he was clueless regarding the Frank's Fuel Oil scam by Mack Mills. I expected him to be furious when he got the news about the fraud, not only for himself, but the rest of the stockholders.

Now that the property had been located, law enforcement needed to be advised and get the ball rolling when the time was right. Trespassing on the land, discovered by me and Cecil would be very dangerous. It was obvious that several vehicles had recently visited the site, flattening saw grass and leaving tire tracks. Not a single clue had been left behind to indicate who was poking around. GPS coordinates would not be reliable without a copy of a survey, which should be available with the deed. The name of the purchaser was unknown, but the underground tanks Cecil and I found confirmed the physical site. There were a lot of unanswered questions.

I knew Kyle and John hoped to find a copy of the deed in Josie's files and no telling what else their mission would turn up to incriminate her

and Mack. Talk about sitting on pins and needles.
Ouch!

Exposing my source, Ginny Faye, was not
going to happen today, but the Chief would
eventually find out who the whistle blower was
after the sting went down. In spite of the variables,
I made the call to the Chief. The dispatcher put
me through.

"This is A. C. King, with some important
information that you need to hear from me in
private. Are you free now?"

"What's up Ace? Can't you tell me over the
phone what's going on?"

"Not good enough. We need complete privacy.
Are you available or not?"

"Look son, you're starting to worry me. Come
on over and tell me what's troubling you. I'll see
you in ten minutes. Give me time to threaten my
dispatcher."

Nine minutes later, his gal Friday pointed a
long manicured nail at the Chief's door directing
me to enter. She didn't speak and she didn't look
happy.

George Herring had proved to be a
conscientious police chief after his land-slide
election two years ago for his third term in office.
His cousin, Sheriff Pat Garrett, had won his
election by tying himself to the Chief's apron
strings. Our sheriff was proving to be sneaky and
snarly and was earning his nickname, The

Weasel. The first thing I did was ask Chief Herring to leave his cousin out of the loop on what I was about to tell him. The last thing I needed was a leak from the loose-lipped sheriff.

"Pat Garrett and I don't see eye to eye on anything," said Chief Herring. "You let that comment leave this office and I will deny I ever said it, but he will not be informed by me. Now tell me, what's got you so riled up?"

I took a long, deep breath before opening my mouth to exhale. " You were upset when I came to you for information earlier this year and you had every right to shut me down, but that did not stop me from looking for answers elsewhere. I found a link in some old court records which led me to Mack Mills through a back door. Shall I continue?"

"Mack Mills? Just exactly what are you getting at son?" Chief Herring was turning his favorite shade of red.

Taking another deep breath, I looked the Chief straight in the eye. "Please don't call me son. I'm an investigative reporter with a lot of pertinent knowledge about crimes currently being committed under your nose and Sheriff Garrett's. You need to hear me out."

"Well get on with it. You have my full attention," he blustered.

"I have proof that Mack Mills committed fraud against you and the other stockholders with help from other people. He lied about the land being worthless, sold the property for cash, and that money was a down-payment for his first truck stop, the one that burned. Want me to go on?"

"There's more?" he asked, sitting up straighter.

"You bet. I found the abandoned site of Frank's Fuel Oil, showing recent visits from multiple tire tracks. The valve covers over the buried tanks have recently been tampered with. Someone has a special key to unlock the covers which is the only way to access those tanks."

"Do you know who paid cash for that land, Ace?"

"I believe the Memphis Mafia purchased the land, but I don't know why. They also loaned Mack money for his current truck stop. Now they have him running a whore house for them. He seems to be in bed with the wrong people."

Chief Herring's eyes narrowed and his expression changed to that of a bull looking at a flapping red cape. He lowered his head and didn't speak for ten long seconds. He was breathing between clenched teeth. Then he exploded.

"The Mafia and prostitution! I had no idea. A con man. That's what he is. A smooth-tongued liar. My gut was right, but I blew it. I sat on my instincts."

His arms were waving wildly and spittle was spraying across his desktop. I closed my eyes against the onslaught, grimaced and waited him out. He was still snorting through his nose like a bull, but he calmed down and didn't gore the messenger so, I decided to tell him more.

"Both truck stop ventures have made Mack Mills a rich man. His second and current truck stop operates as a front for his newest endeavor, prostitution. According to my source, the Mafia loaned him the money to build on the condition that he include a motel to service truckers. I know your jurisdiction ends at the city limits but. . . . "

"Yeah, yeah. You don't trust the sheriff to handle the situation. This is personal for me and my friends, so I do appreciate you coming to me first. Guess there's no point in asking who your source is."

"Not a chance," I said. "You know they will be called as a witness after all this goes down and I intend to protect them as long as I can."

"What do you mean, when it all goes down? Ace, what are you planning?"

"Look Chief, I'm asking you, no, I'm begging you to stand down and trust me for a few days. Lives could be in danger if you go charging out there with a posse and they hide all the evidence. I believe the assassination attempt on Judge Lester during his retirement dinner is also connected to this mess."

"Why in God's name would the Mafia go after Judge Lester? Are you protecting someone else?"

"Not protecting, but proving that someone had a motive based on revenge and exposing that someone as the king-pin of the Mill's mess. Leave it alone now and maybe nobody will get hurt. A private investigator is on to them and I should hear from him any day now with his findings. When a raid is called for, you can lead the charge along side the FBI or TBI or even the sheriff. That will be for you to decide. Mack Mills is small fish compared to the Mafia. Let's bring the sharks down too. Agreed?"

I could imagine the legal wheels turning in Chief Herring's head. He might be as clumsy as a bull in a china shop but he has a good head on his broad shoulders. After all the information he had just heard, he whirled his leather chair so that his back was to me. He appeared to be looking at his dead son's picture while he pondered his options. It felt like the air was being sucked out of the room. When he finally spoke, his voice conveyed great sadness. When he turned around there were tears in his eyes.

After wiping his eyes with his sleeve, he said, "Sorry I made you feel like a kid. You are a man, just like my son who gave his life for this great country. Ben could not afford to go to college after I lost my investment with Frank's Oil Co. Using his college money was a stupid decision. I was only trying to increase the amount so he could go on to graduate school."

My heart broke for him. The depression in the room was stifling. Now it was his turn to stare me straight in the eye and he finally broke the tension.

"As soon I have your evidence Ace, a raid will have to happen. Bring it to me."

Standing up, we shook hands and the deal was sealed.

Chapter 29

Writing, my favorite way of expressing myself before I fell down the rabbit hole at the beginning of June, was taking a back seat to new impulses churning inside me. I yearned to protect Sandra French and her mother from bad people, punish greedy bastards who pimp their sisters, and prosecute thieves who take from the poor. For the first time in my life, I wanted to own a gun. Camelot had ended when the last leaves fell in early November and winter was nipping at my heels.

The power of the written word works for the Bible because it is the truth, and the same power can work for a small town newspaper. My journal was full of stories, ready to come alive. Not quite yet, but soon. Then watch out. I'm planning to expose the lies and I'm not coming alone on my crusade.

* * *

Forever and a day. That's how long it seemed before Kyle Cunningham called me back.

"It's done," he said.

"In the name of Mother Earth and Father Heaven, tell me more than that."

"Later, with a conference call, around eight tonight. Be sitting down. I'm hanging up now."

Again, I was left holding a silent phone. Kyle really needed to work on his communication skills.

* * *

Waiting at home for the conference call was like waiting for eggs to hatch under a brood hen. The cell phone and recorder were plugged in and charging long before the eight o'clock hour arrived. I planned to record every word on tape before the call ended, as well as take notes of the conversation. There would be no do-over available and I wanted to savor every word.

Pacing the floor irritated the carpet and my parents. Somehow, I knew nothing would ever be the same after this call. Reputations and jobs would be affected and I would be connected to law enforcement as a witness. Picking up my journal brought instant calm. Killing time was better than watching a live clock slowly tick.

Precisely at 8 p.m. the phone rang. Snatching it off the table, I answered. "Ace King here. Who's calling?"

"Kyle Cunningham and John Masters."

"Please tell me why you are calling."

"Reporting on our mission, Sir."

"Are you being flip, Kyle?" Someone snickered in the background.

"Relax," said Kyle. "I assume this talk is being recorded and that's good. I'll let John give his blow-by-blow first." Kyle passed his phone to John.

"I entered the truck stop four nights ago after midnight for a dry run. A lonely drunk, who was drinking coffee at the counter, offered me a seat and I joined him. Gave me a chance to scan the room for problems while he blathered. Security surveillance was over the top but I already knew that Mack was thorough from Ginny Faye. She had pin-pointed every camera on the set of blueprints, the obvious and the tiny, hidden ones in his private office and Josie's office. The main security system contained a built-in back-up if disabled for longer than ten minutes, but Ginny Faye knew how to circumvent that. Mack doesn't play double jeopardy for nothing. He had plenty to hide. I had seen enough by the time I finished the cup of Joe."

"Did you find what we wanted?" I asked anxiously.

"Much more. The actual penetration happened last night and was executed with no problems," said John. "I believe the guilty parties can be busted by the county, state or Feds with the evidence I procured. Here's Kyle with details."

Kyle took the phone back. "John and I went over the photos after they were enlarged. They are close-up and clear, and include several weapons.

He re-set the security system, leaving no clues that the offices were invaded. We are in Jackson putting the package together for you tonight before John leaves for Memphis. I will personally deliver the odious photos to you and Ginny Faye tomorrow and go over each document. Of course, John will keep back-up copies in Memphis. Do you have any questions, Ace?"

"Yes. Can I leave you and John in the wind? In other words, is there any reason for your names to come up as witnesses?"

"None at all. Ginny Faye wants to take full credit as the whistle blower and claim she had copies of everything before the divorce. This was her idea, not mine, but I agree with her after seeing the photos John took. He and I wore gloves when we handled the evidence, but Ginny Fay did not wear gloves. Her prints have to be there, in case a smart attorney looks for loop-holes or doubts her integrity. They will have no cause to suspect a break-in. Any other questions before we meet?" said Kyle.

"What time tomorrow and where?"

"Two o'clock. Pick me up in front of the Piggly-Wiggly, behind the State Patrol Headquarters. Ginny Faye's neighbors should be at work, but wear a suit and bring an empty brief case so it will look like a couple of estate planners are calling."

"Sounds like a solid plan for the exchange. I'll have a temporary tag on the car," I said.

"Yeah Ace, that worked when we first met. I thought you had a different agenda until we talked. You went from stalker to reporter. Glad we met. See you tomorrow."

He hung up.

Chapter 30

Getting possession of that evidence was all I could think about after Kyle and John's call. Telling Mom and Dad where the investigation had taken me was liberating. For my drive to Jackson the next day, Dad insisted I use a black Lincoln Continental off the car lot that he had recently purchased at an auction. He assured me the license plate would not be a temporary tag, but a special issue that looked very official. Mom suggested I should wear black sunglasses and offered to shine my black shoes. My parents were as anxious for the revelation of the documents as I was.

* * *

The suits, sunglasses and car elevated me and Kyle to "Men in Black" status. We sauntered up to the front door with our brief-cases, looked each other up and down and nodded our approval at the transformation..

Ginny Faye flung open the front door as soon as we rang the doorbell, acted surprised and asked, "What do you nice looking men want today?"

"A moment of your time. Are you the lady of the house?" said Kyle.

"Why, yes, I am. Are you here to help me plan my estate with some new money that I'm about to come into?"

That did it. We all burst out laughing as Ginny Faye motioned us to step over the threshold and get down to business. The coffee table was clear. No sweet tea or cookies would be served today.

Snapping open his case, Kyle revealed the secrets that Mack Mills and Josie Cagle thought were hidden from the world. He spread the documents out in long rows across the table. We were sitting on the sofa, shoulder to shoulder, bent forward and staring down. There was more than we had imagined.

The original letter to the stockholders, compiled by Josie and Mack, claiming bankruptcy, was there. A phony deed for the land sale was also there and anyone with a brain should have known it was a fake. The imposter document was deeded to Lucius Hogg from Mack Mills, followed by a bill of sale in the amount of $500,000, paid in full by Lucius to Mack for the land.

A ledger, listing the recorded names of men and the amount of cash rendered for each visit to the whore house was present. Many of the men were repeats, but one stood out. Sheriff Pat Garrett was a regular, leaving only a tip, as compared to the others. His protection apparently afforded him services at a huge discount.

Tax statements did not match balance sheets for any year because there were two sets of books for each year, suggesting tax fraud on the federal and state levels. Cash deposits were spread over six different off-shore account locations in the Bahamas. We were bug-eyed by the time we saw all the levels of deception that John had discovered.

Missing was an original land deed in Frank Mills or Leon Cunningham's name for the fuel oil location. Kyle had gone through his father's papers and found nothing. A search warrant at the family home of Mack Mills, where his mother resided, would now be justified.

The FBI would deal with the Memphis Mafia, depending on what evidence was found in the oil tanks when they were eventually dug up.

A late night raid at the truck stop would bring down the dynasty created by Mack and Josie. They would be facing years in prison with a long list of charges from state and federal authorities. Carefully gathering the spread of damning information, I placed the papers in the empty briefcase that I had brought to the meeting.

I turned to Ginny Faye and asked, "Do you still want to be a witness against Mack?"

"Absolutely," she said with no reservation. "And even more against Josie. She helped elevate my husband to a criminal by holding him hostage with proof of fraud, money laundering, tax evasion and prostitution that she secretly locked away. Now they need to be locked away for a long time and account for their choices."

Turning to face Ginny Faye, Kyle asked, "You know you have to do this without my testimony or John's. Can you take the heat?"

With a toss of her head, she said, "I'm a professional chef. If I could not take the heat, I would have gotten out of the kitchen a long time ago."

Chapter 31

Leaving Jackson with enough evidence from my spies to conquer a small country was nothing short of victory. The deal that I had made with Chief Herring had to be fulfilled today and I was pumped and ready.

The Lincoln Continental floated me home on Interstate 40, past the truck-stop with a brothel, past the old billboard with all its complexities, past the exit for Chiggerville State Park, crossing the Tennessee River bridge and finally arriving at the Turtle Creek exit. This odyssey, that began for me in June would be over before the end of the year.

* * *

First things first. Return Dad's car at his sales office. Handing him the keys when he turned around caused him to pause and process the man in front of him. I was wearing black sunglasses, a power tie with a black suit, shiny black shoes and holding a brief case.

"What have you done with my son?"

A parent with a sense of humor is priceless.

"Dad, you will not believe what is in this briefcase. Ginny Faye wants to testify against her ex-husband and the Memphis Mafia is going down too. Excuse me now, but I'm in a hurry to get this in the hands of Chief Herring. See you at dinner." For once in my life, I left my dad speechless.

* * *

I breezed across the street, ignoring beeps on my way to the Police Station. The Chief was standing outside, saw me coming with the fat briefcase and held open the door. I never broke stride. We almost collided in front of the dispatcher when we tried to enter his office together. He was eying my briefcase like it was the 'ark of the covenant'.

"Tell me that's what I think it is?" he asked.

"A deal is a deal. Congratulations Chief. Who else should we call for this unveiling? The D.A. for sure and the FBI. Oh, and don't forget TBI when it's time to raid the sons-a-bitches. This is just a suggestion, but I would leave the sheriff out altogether since he's listed in a little black journal as a regular visitor to the whore house."

Raising his eyebrows in surprise, he said, "You have got to be kidding." The chief paused to digest the brevity of this information, then summed it up. " Well, the weasel deserves what he gets."

"One more thing, Chief. I believe that I have earned the exclusive right to report on this sting first, so how about letting me ride with you?"

"I would be proud to give you credit for the whole operation. You have my word. Now explain this evidence so I can sort out which posse to call for what."

An hour later, the Chief had reviewed and understood what I had brought him. After calling the D.A. to set up an emergency meeting, he called Judge Lester.

"Are you staying in town for the next few days? Yeah, well that's good news. I'm gonna need a couple of search warrants, so stand by. Look, I can't tell you what's going down, but it's big. After I meet with the D.A., to show him a pile of evidence that just materialized, I will fill you in. Gotta go. Call you back soon."

* * *

Walking out of the Police Department with an empty briefcase left me full of relief. Swinging the case, I hot-footed to the Gazette to give Loretta a heads-up that a news story was about to split the county wide open. I told her it would be an exclusive for our paper and extra copies would need to be printed next week. She was ecstatic.

* * *

Winter arrived in late November with a vengeance. Lows in the 30's would be dropping into the teens at night driven down by north winds. Anyone who did not have to go out stayed parked in front of their fireplaces or stoves. Law enforcement was an exception. The date of the prearranged raid on the truck-stop was nonnegotiable and would happen on the worst night of the year. I borrowed Dad's impregnable parka and insulated gloves, reserved for the coldest Tennessee home football games. Mom produced a pair of smart-wool socks, meant to be one of my Christmas presents and I was touched and grateful.

Scheduled for 8 p.m., when traffic was lightest on Interstate 40, law enforcement raided the truck stop. The Tennessee Bureau of Investigation, with a well rehearsed task force of heavily armed men, led the way. Chief Herring did not involve Sheriff Pat Garrett, who would be forced to resign later, otherwise he might have become suspicious and squeal to Mack and Josie. Five vehicles descended on the truck stop with flashing lights including the State Highway Patrol.

There was no resistance and no one got hurt. Three girls on the job were taken into custody for soliciting prostitution, as well as their johns who refused to identify themselves. The offices of Mack and Josie were unlocked, then looted by the search party. The contents of their files were seized along with their computers and several weapons. I recorded our arrival, entrance and removal of evidence on video. No crime tape was hung across the front doors, but a simple 'closed sign' was put on the doors temporarily and the few hardy souls who were out that night quickly vacated the parking lot. Lowly personnel were warned not to notify anyone and sent home. Orange cones were placed at the entrance ramp to the truck stop along with a state trooper in his warm car. He would vacate when the next shift of workers arrived, allowing the public to access the gas pumps again. The raid took less than thirty minutes.

PART IV

Southern Happenstance

Chapter 32

A search party of two local deputies knocked on Mrs. Mill's front door, rousing her from sleep, scaring her half to death. They showed her a warrant, went to work and found the land contract they were told to look for as soon as the old lady opened the safe. Buried on the bottom of a yellowed pile of papers, lay an expired lease, between Frank Mills, Leon Cunningham and the state of Tennessee for the fuel oil business. The men bowed out with an apology, taking the incriminating contract with them. Mrs. Mills was confused, worried and needed to talk to her son.

Mack and Josie were having a heated argument that night when his mother tried twice to phone. Mack ignored the first two attempts that she made to contact him. By the time he answered her third call, he was pissed. Josie had left the room to go to the bathroom, heard the phone ring, but that's all she heard.

"What the hell do you want Mother?"

"They came to my house and took things out of the safe. I was so scared they would hurt me. Can you please come to my house right now?" she pleaded.

Jumping to conclusions, Mack thought his mother had been robbed. He grabbed his coat and left without telling Josie where he was going. When Josie came out of the bathroom, he was backing out of the driveway.

Her negative reaction was barely short of the boiling point, leaving no room for common sense. Assuming the call was some stupid emergency at the truck stop, which happened all the time, she decided to follow and give him a piece of her mind. Too angry to realize that Mack had taken the truck, she stumbled around the house in search of her ring of keys. Zipping her leather jacket up tight and pulling on her deer skin gloves was habit. She failed to notice the wool scarf on a hook beside the door. The black helmet with a face shield would do the trick and a flask of Jack Daniel's whiskey was always in one of the Harley's side packs.

Having a tryst in the office late at night was wicked fun. She would surprise him, and they would finish off the half-pint together. Afterward, she would leave the cycle at the truck stop and they would ride home together. The nightly drinking, which had fueled her latest fit of rage at Mack, was ebbing away, being replaced with the reality of the sobering cold night air.

Upon approaching the off ramp to the truck stop, Josie saw flashing lights and orange cones and knew something was wrong. She idled closer to the parked patrol car intending to ask if she could go further, but was met with an outstretched arm when the trooper got out of his car.

"What happened here? An accident?

"No lady, a raid happened. This stop is closed for the next hour. I am here until the night shift shows. You will find a rest stop about seven miles from here. Sorry."

"Sorry my ass. It's half frozen. I need a warm restroom. Can't you just let me go in for a few minutes?"

"Where are you headed on a cold night like this riding a cycle?" he retorted.

Lying easily, Josie said, "Jackson, but it's too far in these conditions and I have to go back home. I never saw the weather report before leaving. Please, I just have to pee and warm my hands before I turn around."

Unseasoned troopers have a soft spot for women in distress. This one was no different and he granted her request. "Ten minutes lady. I expect to see your tail-light leaving."

"Thanks officer." Josie gunned the black machine forward, hoping Mack had not been caught in the snare. His vehicle was nowhere to be seen and that could either be a good or bad sign. Peering through the glass doors showed no activity or personnel in view. A "Temporarily Closed" sign was strung across the entrance. Using her key for a quick entry, she headed for the ladies room in what appeared to be a deserted space. Even before warming up with the hot air blowers, she tried to call Mack, but he had turned his phone off to block her calls after leaving. Cursing him raised her anxiety level and warned her to get out before she was recognized. Where was Mack? Maybe someone tipped him off about the raid. She heard a phone ringing somewhere in the back where the offices were, but was too afraid to stay in the building any longer or leave a message on Mack's phone that someone else might hear. Suddenly, the toilet seat felt like a block of ice. She panicked and quickly left the building.

Mack knew a red herring when it flopped in front of him. His mother's home had not been robbed, but raided with a search warrant, probably by TBI, looking for some specific document to bring down his house of cards. She was as clueless as he was about what they took. Should he be worried? Hell yes. He called the truck stop repeatedly, getting no answer. When no one answered the phone, he knew. A raid with a bigger net had been cast over the primary location, his business. He couldn't go there, but he had to go home and warn Josie before they were arrested.

Racing out the front door of the truck stop and mounting her faithful steed was when the cell phone trilled in the rear pocket of Josie's jeans. If she had put the helmet on and started the motor, she would have missed the sound and headed back to Turtle Creek.

Fate is a fickle happenstance of life over which we have no control.

Chapter 33

The execution of the raid was a huge success. After Judge Lester heard the evidence that the police chief possessed, he had signed the search warrants with no second thoughts. After the raid, he looked forward to issuing arrest warrants for Mack Mills and Josie Cagle. Little did anyone suspect they were in the wind. Fate had dealt another hand in this game of thrones that was not over yet.

The truck stop opened as usual when the night shift arrived after the raid and the patrolman at the entrance ramp departed, taking his cones with him. No one was an acting manager so the workers cooked, cleaned and clerked like nothing had happened. The big boss, Mack, with his crabgrass personality, seldom made an appearance outside of daylight and his bodyguard bookkeeper was avoided at all cost. The employees played dumb and dumber in regard to the prostitution going on and continued to collect their paychecks while keeping their eyes open for jobs elsewhere. No one was compelled to call Mack out of loyalty or curiosity, but easily turned a deaf ear to the current event. That was unfortunate for Mr. Mills because he needed to know what had gone down before he decided to run. Earlier, when he had called the office, the business phones had not been answered. Another unfortunate moment since Josie was in the building and could have fielded that call. Mack was frustrated beyond belief by the time Josie answered his call to her.

Before he could say a word, she demanded, "Where in hell's name are you?"

"Shut up and listen. I just left mother's house after her safe was cleaned out by those bastards."

"What bastards?"

"Feds, State, the sheriff, I don't know, Josie. They had a warrant and took papers from the safe. You know I don't keep my personal business in mom's house so what the hell were they looking for?"

"Now you shut up and listen to me. I followed you when you took off without a word. Thought you were going to the truck stop. That's where I am now, you damn fool. They were here. Hordes of cops. Gone now, with everything. Shut us down. Took the girls, too. They might come back and catch me here alone."

Mack was grimacing and grinding his teeth as she laid it out for him. The D.A. could be ready as early as tomorrow morning to have arrest warrants issued. Time for him to get out of Dodge.

"You will have to dump the motorcycle somewhere. I'll pick you up after I swing by the house to get our passports and some clothes. We can get ahead of them and fly out of Memphis tonight. Good thing my money is in the Bahamas."

"Good? Are you frigging crazy, Mack? I am half frozen with no warm place to hide. Staying here at the truck stop is not an option. So how do you plan to get me out of this mess? Do not even think about leaving me behind or I will turn state witness and burn your sorry ass. Then I'll tell the Mob where your mother lives. You should have told me where you were going in the first place."

Josie's outburst of vicious threats was not lost on Mack and he was scalded to the bone. God knows he was sick of her drunken hissy fits. Why did she have to screw everything up by leaving the house to follow him like the bitch she was? In that second, she became a repulsive liability and he hated her. Mack tasted bitters on the back of his tongue and knew her usefulness to him had ended. He did not even care what happened to his mother, since he had enough money to live well for the rest of his life and even richer if he left alone.

Lying words poured out of his mouth to calm and seduce the wicked witch of the south. Mack intended to buy some time, getting a head start on his escape. As they spoke, he was backing out of his driveway with a packed carry-on.

"Stay where you are for fifteen minutes. Hide in the restroom if you must. I'm pulling in the driveway now," he lied. "I can grab what we need and be gone in a few minutes. When I get to the Interstate, I'll call. Then you can ride to the vacant lot, dump the bike and I'll meet you there. Think you can handle the cold for a few more minutes?"

"What choice do I have?" she growled back.

I have a better choice without you, he thought, as he headed out of town.

"And screw the clothes," she shouted, "Just grab the passports. That's all we need with a credit card and your wad of cash."

Mack disconnected the conversation as he vowed to never let another woman ruin his life again. "Screw them all," he said aloud.

Twenty minutes later he called Josie back, keeping the pretense alive. Keeping his voice calm, he instructed her to leave the truck stop and meet him at the designated rendezvous, assuring her that his arrival would be shortly. By now, the master liar was approaching Jackson, on old Hwy.70 and less than one hour away from freedom. American Eagle in Memphis would accommodate him with a late flight to New Orleans. From there he could disappear.

The Tennessee State Trooper noticed the red tail-light on the cycle as Josie left the truck stop going west. Then she turned left to cross the overpass and left again to go east on the Interstate. He was curious about the woman and her motive for the outwardly unnecessary trip. The stupid things people did had ceased to amaze him. Oh well, he would be off duty and home in bed before the eleventh hour.

Josie took the Buzzard Cave exit and knew that the dirt road, normally muddy, would be solid from the deep freeze. Mack was not there, but she assumed he needed a few more minutes. She hated to abandon her beloved bike. Leaning it against a small tree, she lowered the kick stand and extracted the contents from the leather packs. Taking a long swig of the Jack Daniel's whiskey was welcome and warming to her insides. Like a deer being felled by one shot, the bike fell over with a thud. Surprised, she up-righted and re-set the kickstand, wondering if this night would ever end. As the minutes ticked by, she thought Mack was later than he should be. Impatient, she called him but the ring went straight to voice mail. She drank some more of the whiskey before calling again. No answer. Slowly an alternate truth dawned. *Maybe he left without me.* The alcohol had muddled her brain, but not her instinct for survival. *Have to leave if he's not coming, or meet him on the way out to the exit.* She jerked the bike away from the tree, threw herself on it, but the starter failed to engage the engine. *No, No, NO!* She realized the fall had damaged the mechanics and after repeated tries to revive the dead horse, Josie knew deep down she had been abandoned.

They found her the next day, sitting on the bare ground, leaning against the cycle with an empty pint between her outstretched legs. She was stone-cold dead.

Chapter 34

Curacao, a Dutch island off the coast of South America, claims to have the prettiest turquoise water in the world, with beautiful homes and vacation villas facing the water. There is a port and docks for two cruise ships arriving daily bringing honest tourists and criminals alike. This was the kind of place Mack Mills imagined he would live, but he forgot one important detail when he left Josie behind. She had the passwords memorized for the six off-shore accounts. Damn!

All he had were traceable, therefore useless, credit cards, a passport and a nearly empty money clip. His truck had been abandoned in a satellite parking lot at the Memphis airport before flying to New Orleans and without access to the accounts he was broke. Mack was slumming in a poor parish apartment and working as a dish washer with the constant smell of crayfish and shrimp shells up his nose when the police found him. He was promptly extradited back to Tennessee, jailed in Turtle Creek's fine facility and charged with everything that was applicable. He would spend the rest of his life incarcerated next door to his boyhood home, in the Tennessee State Prison. Very convenient for his mother's visits.

The Memphis mafia did not get off unscathed, it just took a few days to catch up with Lucius and his crew. The three hos, picked up during the raid, were happy to roll over on their pimp, Chickie Smith. He cut his own deal and rolled on the rest of the mob leading to the arrest of Lucius at the Hot Shot Gun Range by the Memphis Police Department. Kelly Cunningham, his gun instructor, who thought he was a very nice business man with a passionate hobby for guns, was shocked and unbelieving. When she complained to her father, Kyle, about the injustice in this world, the Transformer smiled at the idea and wisely told her nothing about his involvement with the sting.

The state of Tennessee brought backhoes to the land site and carefully dug up the fuel tanks, finding plenty of evidence to convict Lucius and his mob for a long time. Contrary to their fears, only one tank was partially filled with oil. A total of 221 burner phones were found in the other three tanks yielding enough information to embarrass the defendants' lawyers into accepting plea deals for their clients instead of suffering through long trials. Several guns found along-side the phones cleared a number of murder cases languishing in the cold case files of the Memphis Police Dept. which led to several murder indictments. The chance of Lucius or his mob getting reduced sentences was zilch.

The Mexican cartel stepped right in to fill the void, believing they had been blessed by the Pope for their restrained patience.

EPILOGUE
Six months later

Sitting in church on a beautiful June day with all my friends and family around is what life is all about. Two amazing women, soon to be stepsisters, pressed against each side of me. The room was full of love and peace because a wedding was about to unite two souls who adored and respected each other. A low hum of conversation and nervous coughs broke the silence until the familiar music began announcing the march of the bride. Ginny Faye was escorted down the aisle on the arm of the Honorable Richard Pruitt, both beaming smiles all the way. Kyle, the happy groom, while awaiting her approach had tears on his face. Looking left and right, my companions also were dabbing their eyes. Odd that God only gave tears to be used for different emotions to humans. Today, they were tears of happiness.

The beautiful ceremony, with vows written by each other, was honest and moving. Kyle held Ginny Faye's face gently with his huge hands to kiss her before they faced the witnesses to be introduced as Mr. and Mrs. Kyle Cunningham. The room erupted in applause and whistles during their walk to the reception hall.

So much had changed in twelve months. This time last year I was sitting in a courtroom instead of a church. Between the two places, I found myself. Now I work for the Nashville Tennessean as a free-lance reporter and investigate cases for Masters Detective Agency out of Memphis. I burn up the "Music Highway" on Interstate 40 in a big black Lincoln Continental, purchased used from the Greyhound Auto Mart with a personalized plate that reads, "Deal Me." After winning a Pulitzer Prize in journalism, I wrote my first novel based on the events of the past year. Positive feedback on the book from my former editor, Loretta, has encouraged me to write a series using stories from my journal.

Maybe you are wondering what happened to the truck stop and all the off-shore money denied to Mack. A national conglomerate purchased the truck stop at public auction and continues to operate to this day. All of the millions were recovered by Ginny Faye with the account numbers and passwords which she had copies of from day one. Giving up the ill-gained money to pay taxes, liens and debts owed, including the initial investments plus interest to the stock holders was natural for her. She gave the remaining balance to the Federal Land and Wildlife Conservation program because she could. All the people touched by Ginny Faye's generosity were at the wedding. All of Kyle's comrades were also in attendance. The honorable Judge Harold Lester II officiated the wedding. He was the icing on the cake.